GOOD-BYE AND AMEN

Other books by Francis Clifford

GOOD-BYE AND AMEN

Published in England under the title
The Grosvenor Square Goodbye

FRANCIS CLIFFORD

New York and London

Harcourt Brace Jovanovich

cop.a
0669

Printed in the United States of America

The extract from a song called "Never, Never, Never" is
printed by permission of Southern Music Publishing Co. Ltd.

Library of Congress Cataloging in Publication Data
Clifford, Francis.
Good-bye and amen.
A novel.
I. Title.
PZ4.T4666Go3   [PR6070.H66]   823'.9'14   74-12182
ISBN 0-15-136630-6

First American edition

B C D E

For my friends
in
Warwick Lane and
Lower John Street, London,
and
East 49th Street, New York,
with many thanks
for their help over the years

If we begin with certainties, we shall end in doubts: but if we begin with doubts, and are patient in them, we shall end in certainties.

—Francis Bacon: 1561–1626

1

DARKNESS

11:59 P.M.

DANNAHAY lifted his eyes off the report, nodding like a man who was thinking hard, and said to Knollenberg: "See if you can get him, Charles."

"Okay."

"You could find we sewed it up tonight."

"Okay."

"No kidding," Dannahay said. "I mean that."

12:00 midnight

GOD knows they had fought before, but never like this.

"Get out!"

Raged and wept and gone wild with each other, but nothing as bad.

"For Christ's sake, get out!"

A hundred times, a thousand times. Fifteen years together. But never so savage, nothing so cruel.

"Bitch," he shouted back at her, a sort of madness in his

eyes as he stormed into the darkness of the waiting night and slammed the door behind him.

The whole house shook. Renata Lander didn't hear him stamp away. She stood with hands clenched in agony at the sides of her head, nothing quite real, the crash of the door as loud in her ears as at the moment of its happening. In the awfulness of the silence that followed she could hear it still, slamming reflexively through all the times before, the years before, between whatever they had been along the way and whatever they were now.

God, oh God, oh God.

Another sound made her turn. Noel was at the bottom of the stairs, pale and scared-looking in his check pajamas.

"What happened?"

"Your father went out."

He blinked at her. Fourteen, and sometimes like a man. But only a kid now, just a kid, raw-eyed and insecure, the world not broken into yet for what was waiting to be learned.

"Before," he said, puberty cracking the voice. "What happened before?"

"You must have heard."

"I didn't."

"We had a row," she said, sick in the stomach and wishing like hell he hadn't come down. "The whole of Bruton Mews must have got it loud and clear."

"Was it you made him mad again?"

"We made each other mad."

"Why?" Bewilderment and bitter hurt compounded. "Why d'you *do* that?"

"Go away," she said. It was like another person talking. "Don't ask me idiot questions."

Too late she saw what it did to him, but she was so far gone in her own distress that she had no room for Noel's. A shadow seemed to heave in her mind as he started back up the stairs,

4

but she didn't move; couldn't. She remained where she was, the room beginning to blur out of focus as tears filled her eyes.

Damn you, Harry . . . Damn you . . .

How long she stayed there she never knew. Time had lost its shape. The violent slam of the door was still jarring her brain, and every slashing phrase they'd wounded each other with was in it too, every enraged word and gesture, every single solitary thing right through from when the first chance retort had hoisted a warning signal to the searing look he'd given her as he'd snatched at the handle of the door and then gone.

"Get out!" Hadn't she wanted it? "For Christ's sake, get out!"

She had no memory of switching off the lights, or what else she did, if anything, before going up to bed. All over she was quivering, and her legs were like lead. Noel had left his door ajar. She pushed it open a little more and spoke to the heaped and huddled shape he'd made of himself.

"I'm sorry, Noel."

No answer, yet he must have been awake. And she couldn't manage anything else. Drained, she turned across the landing to the big bedroom. There, quivering still and in a kind of daze, she undressed and flung herself between the sheets and curled up in an attitude of self-protection.

Later, she heard Harry moving about downstairs. She hadn't slept, though she must have been close to going under when she realized he was back in the house.

A little after half past twelve, this was. Her body tensed again and anger pricked her mind. But she thought: What's the use of any more? I'm asleep. No matter what, I'll be asleep.

She waited, expecting him on the stairs at any second. But he didn't come. Instead, he went out again. Not like the last time, thank God, so he'd simmered down a bit. But he'd gone, even so, quiet as a mouse.

Good riddance, she thought defiantly. Walk it off.

Some of the quivering tension ebbed away. Weariness was pushing through her like a wave now, yet she frowned a little in the darkness as she pressed her face against the pillow, and she cried without a sound escaping her.

Never this bad. Never . . . Oh Christ, the things she'd said.

12:28 A.M.

EDDIE RAVEN waited anxiously in the service alley behind the Sin Nombre restaurant and wondered what the man would give him.

Twenty minutes earlier he had searched the litter bins at Bond Street Underground for enough discarded newspapers to be sure of adequate covering for the night. It wasn't the cold at this time of the year so much as the damp; dew was a bugger.

"Anything'll do," he'd said to the man in a raw voice, and saw with relief the look of pity that usually meant a touch.

He had made three calls before trying the Sin Nombre, all of them a blank—sworn at once, warned once, manhandled once. Pride belonged somewhere back in the blur of the past, and he knew well enough what to expect when he made the rounds. But so long as he didn't finish empty-handed, they could sod themselves.

"Anything. I don't mind."

He wasn't as old as he seemed, or as large and misshapen. Inside the verminous layers of clothing, his maggot-pale body was a wasted sack of bones, and a stubble of beard aged him well beyond his fifty years. Life had crushed him long ago, and his veined eyes were dead at the center. He stood now in the shadows of the service alley behind North Audley Street, a wad of newspapers under one arm, fingering the string that was tied around his buttonless outer coat as if he were a parcel. On his head he wore a soiled balaclava.

"Here," the man said, coming back, the change in his tone suggesting he'd already begun to have regrets. "You can take these."

Two bottles, two bottles of Moroccan red. Eddie Raven grabbed them, quick as a bird. Jesus.

"Thanks, mister."

"Just this once—understand? Never again."

"Thanks, mister."

He padded away and turned past Shelley's Hotel in the direction of Grosvenor Square, exulting. *Two* bottles—and easy at that. Not dregs, either; not someone's leavings.

Fourth time lucky, bleeding lucky . . .

A taxi came out of Upper Brook Street and cut across his front as he made his way toward the Roosevelt Memorial. He shouted after it happily, a bottle in each hand, anticipation already easing the ache in his guts.

A yellow sliver of moon was lifting out of the top of the American Embassy. Eddie Raven clambered over the low surround of the fountain on the right of the statue and stretched himself out, FREEDOM FROM WANT cut neatly in the stone above his head. Then he propped himself on a padded elbow and got to work with the corkscrew he had found one Sunday in Hyde Park and which ever since had served him well in his quest for oblivion.

12:52 A.M.
CONSTABLE PETER YORKE swung the police car south at Marble Arch and went on about the nightingale he'd heard the night before. Tim Dysart, in the radio operator's seat alongside, remained adamantly skeptical.

7

"First week in May?"

"Nothing wrong with that."

"Too early."

"Perhaps this one hadn't read the rules."

"Not Berkeley Square by any chance?"

"Hampstead."

"Bananas," Dysart said to that.

"I heard it all right. No kidding."

"You're an expert, are you? What's the color of a blackbird's eggs, and who killed Cock Robin?"

"I'm not deaf, that's all."

The older man belched quietly. "Blast this indigestion."

They were sharing Park Lane with only a scattering of traffic, cruising within the regulation speed and for a moment unmindful of other people. Then a white Aston-Martin overtook them in the outer lane, powering past at well over seventy, and Yorke drew in his breath as if someone had touched an exposed nerve. He pulled out, accelerating hard, the car's blue flasher blinking.

"What d'you bet he's another flaming Arab," Dysart said, "with a nice line in CD immunity?"

"My blood pressure'd never take it."

"Give it a go."

The Dorchester blurred by. They were through the lights, the Playboy and the Hilton coming up to their left, no need yet for the horn.

"He's wild, whoever he is."

"No Arabs, no Africans, no CD immunity," Yorke said tersely, beginning to gain. "I want a straightforward lunatic with an English mother and father and too much drink in him and no complications."

"Right," Dysart said, watching the needle climb. "I second that."

"It's nice to be agreed on something."

"CIGARETTE?"

Gabrielle Wilding rolled her head from side to side, and Richard Ireland grinned.

"Don't you ever smoke afterwards?"

"You'll never believe this, but I've heard that one before." The girl yawned and brushed a strand of blond hair from her face. "Besides, you ought to know by now what I do and what I don't."

"One thing I know you do," he said, "and it's fantastic."

They were lying naked on the bed in Room 501 at Shelley's Hotel and they'd been there this time for almost an hour. Ireland lit a cigarette for himself and blew a thin jet of smoke at the ceiling. There were three Nolan prints on the walls, all to do with Leda and the swan. The main dimmer switch was almost in the OFF position, and the girl's body was ivory-colored, small-breasted, small-boned, and her limbs were slack, the eyes lazy and satisfied.

Huskily she said: "About tomorrow. What exactly's the position?"

"Today tomorrow or tomorrow tomorrow?"

"You know what I mean."

"There's no rush," he told her. "They don't need me at the studio until early afternoon."

"And then?"

"We'll sort something out."

"I thought you were only wanted for a voice over."

"So I am." He nodded. "The studio's not the problem."

She was quiet for a moment, thinking, watching the smoke curdle in the pinkish gloom. The faint sound of tires whimpering through a turn intensified the surrounding silence.

Then she said: "What are you supposed to be doing right now?"

"Twenty-four hours' location."

"No questions asked?"

"Not this time."

Ash sparked from his cigarette and settled on them both. She yelped softly, squirmed and twisted, hands slapping. And desire resurrected as she moved against him. He held her, with a chuckle, stretching over to crush the stub in the bedside ashtray.

Wide-eyed with astonishment she said: "You must be joking."

"Not that I'm aware."

"But it's only—"

"Shut up," he told her. "You chat too much."

She smeared her mouth away from his. "Take five." She giggled and clucked her tongue like a clapper-board close to his right ear.

1:20 A.M.

CHARLES KNOLLENBERG was sitting in the back of a rented royal-blue Volvo 144 with a camera resting on his knees. The nearside window was wound right down, and the car was right up against the curb in Mount Street, about thirty yards from the entrance to the Vagabond Club.

No one was with him. When he parked the car almost an hour ago, he was careful to position it so that the back seats were in maximum shadow. Since then he hadn't smoked, and only occasionally had he even slightly shifted position. The antiglare blind was dropped over the rear window, and time and again people had come and gone along the sidewalk at less than arm's length without knowing he was there.

"I'll say this," Dannahay had told him once. "You're almost better than a goddamned statue when it suits you."

The camera on Knollenberg's knees was a Hasselblad with a

telephoto attachment, the film was fast and specially uprated to be faster still. He sat with his eyes fixed unwaveringly on the discreet pine door of the Vagabond, tensing slightly whenever it opened and anyone came out. Four times this had happened since he took up position, but the man he was waiting for didn't emerge. The fifth time it was different.

"Good night, sir," a voice said as the door yielded. Seconds later his quarry appeared. *Yes*, Knollenberg's mind snapped, and the camera came up, the street lights full on the man's face as he paused fractionally before turning toward Park Lane.

There was only this one chance, the briefest, and Knollenberg took it, cool as could be. But as he watched the man stride away, and waited a full minute before driving off, he knew Dannahay wouldn't be satisfied with what he'd got. Nowhere near.

1:29 A.M.

RALPH MULHOLLAND saw the thin slit of light under his wife's door and tapped a soft rat-a-tat.

"Mary Kay?"

"Hi," she said, peering over her spectacles. "How'd it go?"

"Fine, just fine. I finished over at Maxwell's place for a nightcap. Didn't figure on your being awake somehow."

"It's quite a book I'm reading."

Mulholland yawned, pulling the knot of his tie apart. He was fifty-seven years old and shaped like a fullback. For more than half his life he had been married to this woman, and there were no regrets.

"How were the speeches?" Mary Kay said.

"Short, thank God, with one exception. You-know-who. And instantly forgettable—mine included, I daresay." He puckered his face. "Twice this week already I've listened to Peterson mouthing platitudes, and I see we're doomed to hear him again on Friday, at the Friends of America—"

"Don't tell me."

"Mary Tudor's reported to have said they'd find 'Calais' written on her heart when she was dead. I'm going to have 'Sir Henry Peterson.'"

"Poor Ralph. I thought maybe he'd change his style tonight, since it was stag."

"Not him. Not a bosom in sight, yet he idn't seem to notice. Just plowed on and on. How the Prime Minister suffers him, I can't understand. He wasn't there, incidentally. He had to cancel—laryngitis."

"You should have that yourself once in a while. Then I might see something more of you."

Mulholland grinned. "Friday, for instance?"

"Why not?" Mary Kay smiled back.

In pretense, he put a hand to his throat, frowning slightly. "You know, I do believe—"

"Better safe than sorry—that's your excuse."

He bent over and kissed her. "Never thought the day would come when you'd try to undermine the duties and intentions of an American ambassador."

"Peterson to you," she said. "Good night, Ralph."

"It's a federal offense. Or aren't you aware of that?"

"Phooey."

"Good night, Mary Kay."

1:47 A.M.

IN THE DREAM, Noel Lander was trying to do one of his father's impressions—the Peter Lorre one, the best he did.

"You see, my friend, I am here to arrange for the—shall we say?—recovery of a certain object which has mysteriously gone

12

astray. A most cherished object, with a value—how shall I put it?—more related to the owner's reputation than his pocket..."

Somehow, in the dream Noel realized it was only a dream. For a reason he couldn't make out, but which wasn't important, they were outside the Lycée Française in the Brompton Road, opposite the Natural History Museum, and quite alone.

His father clapped his hands approvingly and said: "Not bad, not bad."

"Think so?"

"You ought to try some of the present-day crowd. That's more your scene. I can only make out with the oldies—Bogart, Sanders, Cagney, people like that."

"They're the ones I like too."

"You watch too much TV, that's your trouble. All those rerun movies."

Perhaps it was the resonance that made him aware that none of this was real.

"Listen, you," Noel heard himself say. "I'm the guy who makes the deals and decides on the small print—"

"Edward G?"

"Right first time."

"Reckon you'll have to keep him until your voice breaks properly."

The dream went out of him then, just clouded over, and he twitched in his sleep the way a dog does.

1:50 A.M.
"WHAT'S THE MATTER?" Helen Olivares asked her husband, Roberto.

He was perched on the side of the bed in the manager's suite at Shelley's, holding his face, all hunched up.

13

"What *is* it?" she pressed him, suddenly out of sleep and fearing the worst.

"Toothache," he muttered.

"Bad?"

"I am not awake from laughing."

She let it pass. "Have you taken anything?"

"No."

"Anadin? Panadol?"

"No."

"Why not?" She put on a light. "How long've you been like this?"

He used his shoulders as only a Spaniard could. "Ten minutes?" he suggested.

"And you've done nothing about it?"

"I told you."

"God in heaven," Helen Olivares exclaimed. "And you manage a hotel?"

She flounced out of bed, curlers lumping her netted hair, and padded into the bathroom. Thirty seconds later she returned to her husband's side, sympathy not entirely absent from her tone.

"Here—swallow these."

He tilted back his head, features screwed as if he were about to suffer an amputation.

"Where's the pain?"

He pointed vaguely.

"Upstairs? Downstairs?"

"Down."

"Well," she said, "you'll have to stick it until morning. Dentists don't come running in the dead of night, and even if they did, you can bet your life old Gilbert would have a reason for being an exception to the rule."

Roberto Olivares rocked back and forth. His Scottish wife slid under the patterned quilt and checked the time.

"You'll find it's easier in half an hour or so."

"Sure." So matter-of-fact, he thought numbly; so damned matter-of-fact. Sometimes he couldn't understand his wife at all, not one bloody bit. Though one thing was certain: if their positions were reversed, she'd be exactly the same—which was part of the mystery. "Sure," he retorted, bent over in response to a rooted sense of drama. "What's a little thing like half an hour?"

Behind him he heard the rustling of a newspaper. And then she said: "There's nothing here."

He wasn't thinking. "Where?"

"Sagittarians can expect a generally uneventful day tomorrow," Helen Olivares read aloud. "Not a period for gambling or taking any sort of chance. Towards evening it is possible that you may find your social life has a surprise in store, but until next week, when Jupiter . . ."

Her husband groaned in private, eyes tight shut. Incredible.

2:02 A.M.

RENATA LANDER stirred uneasily, slowly becoming aware in the sleeping depths of herself that she was still alone in the bed. And then quite suddenly she was fully conscious, staring at the pillow alongside her own. A thin slice of moon gave all the glimmer there was. She sat up, tossing dark shoulder-length hair as she did so, and reached for the bedside switch, blinking until her eyes adjusted.

Odd . . . She rested her arms on her drawn-up knees and her chin upon her arms, physically still but with her mind picking up speed. *This* late?

On impulse she pulled back the covers and reached for her housecoat. On her way downstairs she glanced into the other bedroom and saw that Noel was out to the world, lying as if he'd tripped and sprawled headlong while on the run. "Why d'you *do* it?" She remembered his expression as vividly as his bewildered tone of voice and was moved now despite herself, closer in spirit to his grief and uncertainty.

She was half expecting to find Harry in the sitting room, curled up on the chintz-covered couch. It had happened before, more times than was good for them both. But no. The lights were still on, but couch and chairs were empty, and she felt a pang that went beyond mere disappointment. She passed through the room into the kitchen and started to make coffee, the past somehow nearer than the present, trying in vain to slow the run of her thoughts.

Some questions the young should never ask their parents and expect a worth-while answer. . . . She waited until the water boiled, then made the coffee black and strong and took it into the sitting room. There—something she rarely did—she lit a cigarette, nervously and without skill, and got smoke in her eyes for her pains.

Harry, she thought, all anger spent. For God's sake . . . Enough's enough.

2:10 A.M.
DANNAHAY'S authority came all the way down the line from where it mattered most at the FBI: this much was accepted fact. The rest wasn't so incontrovertible. It was a matter of opinion, for instance, how closely he resembled McQueen, and one of the rumors put about was that he always slept with his right hand taped to the telephone. Whether this was true or not, when Knollenberg rang him the receiver was lifted off the hook before the second double buzz had time to sound.

"Dannahay." Alert as could be, as though he'd been waiting.

"I got him, John."

"Great."

"Alone, though."

"Aw, hell."

"The other one left earlier."

"How long between the two?"

"Eight minutes."

"Shit."

"I can't control what anyone does."

"He didn't have wind of you?"

"Not a sniff."

"He's smooth, y'know. Like ice. It wouldn't show."

"Never so much as looked my way. And considering the speed and aperture I had to use, the print's all you could have hoped for."

"Okay," Dannahay said. "Let's be grateful for small mercies. You going to bring it around?"

"Only if it won't keep."

"What're you going to do instead?"

"Get some sleep," Knollenberg said, aggrieved, "before sleep gets me."

"Okay," Dannahay said. "No sweat. Morning'll do. See you at nine, huh?"

"I'll be there."

2:44 A.M.

IN THE night porter's cubicle behind reception at Shelley's, Jim Usher extinguished his tenth wet filter stub since he came on duty and cast a lazy eye over an early edition of one of the tabloids. His brother worked as a linotype operator in Fleet Street and always, as a favor, dropped a batch of newspapers off at Shelley's on his way home to Bayswater and bed.

The more instant journalism Jim Usher read the more convinced he became of the gap existing between the reality of the world he knew and the one presented him in print. Like here, for instance; nonsense that was. He'd *heard* the man on

17

radio, and if that was wit, if that was funny-hilarious, then someone needed his head examined. He shook his own sadly and turned the page.

Sometimes, of course, there wasn't any cause for dissent. Every fool knew that spring was in full cry, as the photograph showed, with the flower beds in St. James's Park chock-a-block with tulips and all the chestnut trees heavy with blossom. Fair enough. But to say that Lenny Carmody was an aggressive southpaw, when he'd never once been seen to go forward in his life, was inaccurate rubbish. And even worse was the mention of Richard Ireland, reported to have signed for the lead in a new television series and pictured with his wife, Ruth, above a caption which stated that "happiness and success go hand in hand"—worse because half the people that he, Usher, knew were well aware that Ireland was busy screwing some girl or other up there on the fifth floor. Not for the first time either. And as blatantly as could be, as if anonymity was bad publicity.

A slight sound alerted him, and he peered through the cubicle window at the deserted, brightly lit foyer. Reluctantly he put the newspaper aside, got stiffly to his feet, and walked out from behind the reception desk.

There was no movement anywhere except for him. And already he couldn't remember exactly what the sound had been like. He glanced doubtfully across the great spread of patterned carpet toward the concave semicircle of newsstand, gift shop, cosmetic boutique, and travel bureau, then turned on his heel and moved past the rosewood elevator doors and the wide upward sweep of the staircase. A long bank of flowers formed a base to the rectangular glass wall facing massively onto North Audley Street: in this wall the double entrance doors, with their heavy bronze discuslike handles, were set. Usher stopped when he reached them, arms akimbo, gazing at the sodium-lit street that lay beyond his own pale reflection.

It was as quiet and motionless outside as in. Nothing. No one . . . He pursed his lips and glanced at his watch. A good three hours before the cleaners came. Imagination, that's what it was.

2:53 A.M.
SODDING DAMP . . .

Eddie Raven wriggled angrily under the covering of newspapers, his drugged mind disturbed by the patter of falling water. For perhaps as long as twenty seconds he didn't stir again. Then he grunted and uncovered his haggard face and glared apprehensively about him. His mouth was like a kiln, and there was a pile driver at work inside his head, everything jarring in and out of focus. He couldn't imagine where he was, couldn't remember. But he made an effort and managed to squeeze his vision into a frayed distortion of what was actually in front of him, and what he saw seemed as high as a tidal wave, swaying in the moonlight.

He let out a cry and clambered in panic to his feet, about to stagger away when a terrified backward glance brought him abruptly to his senses.

Fountain . . . Jesus, a fucking fountain.

He rocked incredulously on his heels and grabbed the stone surround to steady himself, the sense of nightmare already gone, a tiny remnant of the person he used to be somehow aware of the ludicrousness of such a situation.

He laughed briefly, a sort of croak. Round the bleeding bend . . . Almost immediately his vision lost its sharpness again and anger thudded back into his head. He lurched forward and ducked his face under the water. Mumbling, he then returned to the scattered layers of newspaper and gathered them clumsily together. The two wine bottles distracted him at this point, and he held them aloft, squinting up at each in turn before flinging them furiously across the grass in front of the memorial.

He stretched himself out, wrapping the newspapers about him as best he could. But sleep wasn't going to be easy a second time, and he knew it. The glow of the wine had passed away, and all he'd got left were the beginnings of a hangover and the old desolation.

3:06 A.M.

"TWELVE HOURS from now," Constable Yorke said, making a slow zigzag through the miniature labyrinth of Shepherd Market, "and I reckon the worst'll just about be over."

"How many bridesmaids there going to be?"

"Three."

"Never been best man before?"

"No."

"Nothing to it, really."

"So everyone says."

"Stand up, speak up, and shut up—that's the advice I was given."

"When did you go through the hoop?"

"When I was married," Dysart said, nearer to his own particular version of a smile than Yorke remembered him all night. "Took years to live it down, believe me." He paused a shade, as if for effect. "Did it the hard way. Couldn't remember my wife's name. Got to my feet, opened my mouth and—bing! Paralyzed, I was. Numb."

"I don't think I want to hear."

"You'll never be that bad. Nobody's had a disaster like mine

—not since wedding receptions were invented." A cat raced out of the shadows. "Mind you, from then on things could only get better. If a marriage can survive that, it'll survive anything."

"You've got a point there."

Yorke braked in front of a small bow-fronted shop positioned at the next tight corner. Doors and windows were protected by antitheft steel mesh. Lettered in gilt on the dark-green fascia was: RUSSELL * GUNSMITH. Dysart left the car and tested the locks, the pigeon decoys and binoculars and cartridge belts briefly illuminated by the beam of his flashlight as he flicked it back and forth.

"One fine night," he said, returning to the passenger seat, "someone'll take that little place apart." He was thick about the thighs from too little exercise. "IRA, I shouldn't wonder."

"Just a feeling?"

"That kind of thing."

They came smoothly past the side of the Curzon cinema and turned left.

Yorke said: "He's very security-minded, Russell is."

"Maybe," Dysart admitted. "But you know how it goes. You get this sort of sixth sense nagging away."

"You got one now?"

"On and off."

"Let's hope it's wrong," Yorke said, shifting up a gear. "Nothing along those lines tonight, please God. My tomorrow's all wrapped up and taken care of. I want to be off this stint at seven sharp."

The radio sent a third voice into the car. "Eagle One, Eagle One—are you receiving?"

"Hark, hark," Dysart muttered, "the dogs do bark." He reached for the handset and depressed the button. "Hallo, Alpha Control, this is Eagle One. . . ."

21

3:30 A.M.

RICHARD IRELAND watched in disbelief as the door handle moved. He saw it turn, one way, then the other, very slowly, and he lay on his side and observed it happening as if he were mesmerized. The ceiling light was still on, dimmed right down, but he was facing the door and he wasn't mistaken.

For a moment, to begin with, he thought he *must* be wrong; dreaming, even. But no. By chance he was wide awake. The white alloy knob was being twisted with unnerving caution, and he could hear a faint scratching sound.

Sweat prickled his forehead, ice and fire. The bolt was on, he saw, and the key was in the lock, its tag dangling down.

Seconds elapsed. Then the scratching came to an end, and the handle stopped turning. Ireland held his breath, every muscle in his body rigid with tension. Frantically he wondered what to do—whether to call out, whether to snatch up the phone, whether to rush the door and confront whoever was there. But in the end he did none of these things— not then. Action then was beyond his powers. He couldn't steel himself to move. He remained where he was, how he was, straining his ears and with his gaze riveted straight ahead, fear scampering around his mind and paralyzing his will.

A couple of minutes stretched into an interminable length of time, Gabrielle's breathing the only sound. Finally he snatched for the light switch and plunged the room into darkness, putting an end to the sense of being observed. An enormous effort had been required.

Gabrielle stirred and said thickly: "What's going on?"

"Nothing . . . Nothing."

She probably never heard his reply. Ireland delayed, then slid cautiously out of bed and tiptoed across to the door, a weakness in his belly as he stood with his head close and

22

held his breath and tried to listen above the faulty thunder of his heart. Who came snooping at bedroom doors in Shelley's at dead of night? One thing was sure: he wasn't opening up to find out. And he wasn't going to call the night porter. Most probably it *was* the porter, on his rounds, in which case he'd be making a song and dance about nothing.

His right ear was an inch from the door, his hair just touching. Gone, he told himself. Gone, whoever it was. Adjusting to the darkness, he could make out the handle, and it remained motionless. He waited a little while more, bent-kneed as if on a slack wire, then straightened up and made a silent retreat. When he settled in beside the girl again and felt her warmth, he found that he was trembling. The trembling lasted for quite some time, beyond his control, and he thanked Christ she was asleep and hadn't witnessed the way he'd been—and was even now.

That wasn't the public image at all.

3:41 A.M.

SHIRLEY BASSEY sang softly in the house in Bruton Mews, so effective with that gabbled style she had made all her own, her voice coming from somewhere out of Europe.

> *. . . impossible to live with you.*
> *But I know*
> *I could never live without you.*
> *For whatever you do,*
> *I never, never—*

Renata Lander snapped the radio off, suddenly conscious of the words, an aching hurt touched on the raw. She was drinking her third cup of coffee and half a dozen cigarette ends were crushed untidily in the nearest ashtray. A part of her was leaden with fatigue, yet she was quite unable to settle, fretting, thinking back, thinking forward, pulled in a dozen different directions.

And wondering, question marks galore.

The photograph on the bookcase was as fresh-looking as the day they'd put it in the frame. But he'd changed since then. She'd changed herself as well. Of course. Everyone changed, everyone and everything, inside and out. Fifteen years was a long time, and change was the one inevitability about living. He drank more now, particularly since Ankara. Talked less, at least to her. And could flare into a rage which sometimes had her close to being scared. As he had at midnight . . . and only the other day. Things were different now, all right. They had never been less than pretty tempestuous, even at the start, but laughter was always quick to follow when they came to the boil. They were two of a kind then.

She lit another cigarette, deep within herself yet alert for the sound of his key in the lock. Wanting it, willing it.

Love was most nearly itself when here and now had ceased to matter. Long ago she had learned the truth of that—before Ankara, before Catherine Vanson almost messed everything up. He could still be tender and considerate, could still show glimpses of the way he used to be; but too often during these past few months something got in the way, and he barricaded himself behind it, or drank, or blew his top.

Why? The job was fine; he said so. London was fine; he said so. He liked London. And there wasn't anyone else. No need to have him tell her that; she knew. So why? There were tensions now inside the house that were never around before. Only with Noel did he seem able to relax. It was a joy and a wonder to see them together, to hear the small talk and the banter and listen to their stupid games. There was hope for them all in a bond like that.

Where, in God's name, could he be at this time of night?

Nerves drove her downstairs. Damned if she was going to

ring people round: *then* the tongues would really start to wag, and once was enough for that—Catherine Vanson once. She checked the front door and looked into the garage—no reason for doing so, because he hadn't taken the car, but looking just the same.

"For Christ's sake, get out!" The sound of it was with her still.

The car was there and he wasn't in it—a possibility that struck her only at the moment of putting on the lights. Vaguely, in a second's flash, she clutched at the notion that, rather than venture upstairs, he might have bedded down in the car when he came back into the house again that time.

Wrong. Stupid even to have believed it possible. For one thing, he'd removed his jacket from a chair in the sitting room, and he'd also lifted ten pounds from the kitchen; they kept it there as an emergency stand-by. An hour ago she'd noticed the money was gone, and ever since had tried not to think how ominous it was.

Renata Lander frowned, a flurry of panic at the edges of her mind. On the stairs she said aloud and like a prayer: "I love you, Harry—d'you hear?"

4:07 A.M.

THE DUTY INSPECTOR apologized. "Sorry about that, sir."

"Can't be helped. False alarm's a false alarm."

"Will you bunk down again?"

Detective Chief Superintendent McConnell fingered his black tie and said he wasn't sure.

"Once I'm into my clothes," he said, smiling, "I'm good for the next twelve hours."

"Very well, sir."

He left the Control Room at New Scotland Yard and returned along the corridor to his office, with its tidy desk and hurriedly abandoned camp bed. He was an athletic-looking man, tall, square-shouldered, light on his feet. He wore the black tie out of respect for a sergeant he had known for years who was killed three days before in a bank raid hit-and-run. Out of a tin on the desk he took a peppermint and bit on it, then settled down to drafting a letter of condolence to the sergeant's widow. In David McConnell's book there was never any time like the present, and every word would carry the weight of complete sincerity.

Violent death was always an abomination. Always, no matter whose. Thirty years' service had done nothing to blunt his sensibilities or this belief. One day there would be an alternative to violence, though God alone knew when and what it might be. The world needed mercy most of all.

"Dear Mrs. Stockwell," he wrote, then paused and stared out the soundproofed window. Incredible how early the dawn began to show itself these mornings. Not a quarter after four and already the eastern sky was smeared like gun smoke.

4:20 A.M.

"I'M TELLING YOU," the croupier said, "that's how it was."

Dannahay fingered his fox-red stubble. "Fantastic."

"He finished way in front."

"How much?"

"Six, seven hundred."

"Fantastic," Dannahay said again. "Talk about two birds with one stone."

The croupier had one of those faces that seemed to have gone out of date, the kind El Greco must have known—narrow and sallow and somehow unmarked. Dannahay figured he had the longest, leanest fingers he'd ever seen, like spider's legs with rings on.

"How long was he there?"

"Forty minutes."

"With the Libyan at the table all the time?"

"Except at the end. The Libyan left first, like before."

Dannahay nodded. In front of him was a handwritten record of one person's pattern of play—stakes used and numbers bet on. He glanced down the two columns, which constituted a coded message, and whistled softly. Six or seven hundred profit in addition—how about that? There wasn't any justice.

"Towards the finish he seems to have spread his bets a little—right?"

"Right."

"Was that when he struck lucky and cleaned up?"

The croupier shook his head. "He won early. At the finish he always plays the same, *cheval* and *carré*, on the line."

"Irrespective?"

"That's right."

The croupier stood in Dannahay's apartment with a light raincoat hanging loose over his tuxedo, ready to go, ready to stay. Dannahay didn't believe he'd ever seen the man blink, not once.

"Well, thanks," Dannahay said pointedly. Shit, he was tired. "I reckon that's about it for now."

"How many more times you going to want me to keep this kind of check?"

"Not so many. Maybe just once more."

He started for the door. The envelope was on the ledge in the hallway, and the croupier picked it up as he passed.

"G'night," Dannahay said to him. "*Ciao.*"

4:48 A.M.

EDDIE RAVEN was right about not getting back to sleep again. Because of birds now, twittering away. What with them and

27

all the other din it was a bloody stupid place to have bedded down. Never again. Unless you went underground you couldn't hide from the birds and the racket they made, summer particularly, but the last thing he'd ever want for company another time was piddling fountains.

He sat on the steps that went around the Roosevelt plinth and stared with leaden eyes across Grosvenor Square. Darkness had all but gone. Almost opposite, over at the Indonesian Embassy, they had forgotten to take down their flag, and it hung limp and motionless in the still air.

Dawns by the hundred had found Eddie Raven with a griping pain deep in his guts and the recurring question in need of an answer—where to go next, what to hope for. He lifted his aching head and decided he didn't like the look of the sky. Sod it, he thought; rain now would cap everything. So he pushed himself up, the remains of mittens on his hands, broken boots to walk in. By the nearest tree he searched down through the layers of clothing wherein he existed and pissed gently on the grass.

There was a sickness in his throat like bile as he finished and lurched away, making for Marble Arch. He knew a place or two at Marble Arch that were sometimes good for a touch when the morning got properly under way. He could find a corner until then. Somewhere dry, with no bloody birds and all.

Cars could be a bastard in Grosvenor Square, but not at this hour. Eddie Raven crossed just off the stripes, weaving a little, aiming himself at the eastern corner of North Audley Street. The sky seemed to be growing a little lighter all the time. Diagonally ahead of him, several floors up on the outside fire escape at the end of Shelley's Hotel, a sudden stabbing flash became his final separate awareness.

Then the bullet reached him and ripped him open and everything exploded into the last oblivion of all.

DAWN

HELEN OLIVARES jerked out of sleep and sat bolt upright. "What was that?"

"What was what?" Roberto countered.

"Didn't you hear?"

"Someone backfired, you mean?"

She swung out of bed and went to the nearest window. The manager's suite at Shelley's was on the fourth floor, and the views were limited. Squinting downward she could see into the hotel's service area and, more obliquely, the crisscross of narrow streets a little farther west.

"What else was there to hear?" Roberto wanted to know.

"I couldn't say."

The street lights cut bright straight slots through the greyness of Mayfair's coming dawn, but nothing moved where she could see, not a car, not a person.

"Like something snapping," she thought aloud, breath condensing on the glass.

"A backfire."

"You heard it, then?"

"I told you I heard it," Roberto complained. "I've been awake since God knows when."

She faced into the room's semidarkness with a frown and saw that he was propped up on a stack of pillows. She had forgotten about his toothache.

"No better?"

"Yes and no."

Her nostrils flared a little. With a rising inflection of surprise she said: "What've you been drinking?"

"Bacardi."

She switched on a bedside lamp and studied him, curlers still in her hair, amusement in her half-asleep eyes. A glass and bottle were beside him.

"You look like a drunk."

He shrugged. "The pain's nicely at arm's length."

"And you sound like a commercial." She yawned and rejoined him. "Is that what it was, d'you think? A backfire?"

"Of course."

"Seemed in the room, almost. Right up close."

Roberto grunted. "Not to me."

"The way you are," she said, "I doubt if you'd be considered a reliable witness."

"Not jumpy, though. Not like some people I could mention."

"Listen to who's talking. . . . You'll be in the *Guinness Book of Records* yet."

"What for?"

She turned on her side. "Shortness of memory."

4:54 A.M.

BEN HALIFAX had never discovered who the dog belonged to or where it came from or where it went afterward. It was a brown, big-eyed mixture of Labrador and anyone's guess.

For almost two years now the dog had joined him as soon as he brought the small milk truck into Duke Street. "Chunky," Halifax called it, and it followed him with single-minded devotion up as far as Park Street and all the way round to Carlos Place.

For what? Three or four bread rolls, that was for what. Halifax had no illusions. Yet on the handful of mornings when Chunky failed to make an appearance, he missed him. Funny, that.

"Chunky!"

The dog bounded alongside, and he tossed it the second roll of the morning. Without stopping he nosed out into Grosvenor Square and started to circle clockwise, an almost full load of bottled milk jiggling in plastic crates behind him, the electric-powered truck whining along at its walking-pace maximum.

Time was when Halifax needed to consult his service book for every point of call, but not any longer. Give or take a weekly change or two, he had the entire round off by heart—shops, houses, restaurants, hotels, embassies; Mayfair had them all, cheek by jowl. Crooning to himself, he headed for Upper Grosvenor Street. Best time of day this was, given the weather. No traffic to worry about and the colors just beginning to come back into everything. Half the people he knew said he was out of his mind to do this job, but they were stone-dead wrong.

Chunky had wandered off to the right, across the front of the American Embassy. Idiot dog. He looked to see where it had got to and noticed it was fussing around something lying in the road. Normally Halifax wouldn't have bothered; the distance and the half-light combined to minimize his curiosity. But then Chunky did something he had never known it to do before.

It barked. Not just once, but repeatedly. And in a weird fashion, with its head lifted up and its front legs planted on whatever it had found.

"Chunky!"

The barking continued, something elemental about the whining in between. Halifax slowed the truck to a halt, peering, unable to make out anything in detail. For about ten seconds he delayed, on a tightrope of uncertainty; then the dog whimpered again and raised its snout and let out a couple of almost falsetto snapping sounds. That decided him. Bonehead, he thought, and turned the truck through a right angle. He'd have to go full-circle round the square now, but no matter.

To begin with, he hadn't a notion what Chunky was so worked up about. Even at twenty yards or so he wasn't in the least sure, though the thing was bigger than he'd supposed. Then, suddenly, alarm fingered his spine and he thought he knew.

Jesus.

A moment later he was certain.

"Jesus"—aloud this time.

He brought the truck alongside the body. The dog had stopped barking, but it continued to stand guard, ears flattened, ill at ease. The silence was uncanny. Halifax dismounted and went down on one knee, not liking the feel of what he touched.

"Get off, Chunky. . . . Get off, d'you hear?"

The body was face downward, and he turned it over. The thin stubbled face that presented itself already bore the ageless calm of the dead, but the stench was foul and the sight of the blood took Halifax's senses unawares. Chunky nosed in closer, and he shoved it savagely away. His thoughts seemed to be trying to go in several directions at once. He stood up and looked about him, not knowing what he was looking for,

32

shocked and nauseated and telling himself he needed help. The truck was between him and Shelley's, and it probably saved his life. With a splintering screech, a torrent of milk suddenly burst from the center of his load. He flinched instinctively, and a fragment of a second later the sound of the shot reached him. Like a fool he turned, gaping up at the hotel, and almost at once a second shot thudded into the framework of the truck just beside his head.

Panic entered him then. He started to run, anywhere, anywhere to get away, and Chunky went with him, no bread roll this time but enjoying the novelty and unexpectedness of a game.

4:58 A.M.

FOR SOME REASON, Jim Usher didn't hear the shot that did away with Eddie Raven. But he heard the others just as he was pouring himself an early cup of tea. In the enclosed space of the porter's cubicle they sounded muffled; but close, fairly close. He went at once to the front entrance and pushed out through the glass doors into the coolness of the morning.

North Audley Street had nothing unusual to show, but as he glanced both ways someone opened a window on the third floor diagonally across the street and a head was poked out. This was in the Navy Building, on the corner, and two or three other windows were lit up almost simultaneously at different levels.

It wasn't imagination, then.

"Alpha Control calling Eagle One . . . Alpha Control calling . . ."

Dysart took it.

"Eagle One receiving. Over."

"Man reported shot in Grosvenor Square close to junction

33

with North Audley Street. Alarm call received from duty officer at American Embassy. Suggestion is that shooting may have come from Shelley's Hotel in North Audley Street. . . . Over."

"Roger, Alpha Control. Eagle One proceeding Grosvenor Square immediately. Out."

They were passing Buckingham Palace, the last of the stars competing with the coming day. Yorke put his foot down, and they felt a surging pressure in the small of their backs.

"North Audley's one way."

Yorke said tersely: "So was I till a moment ago."

"Never know your luck." Dysart stifled a belch. "Could be someone playing games."

"Want to bet on it?"

Somewhere in the distance Usher thought he could hear the sound of running. Otherwise it was dead quiet. Away to his right, fifteen or twenty yards past the one-way signs that directed traffic entering Grosvenor Square, he saw Halifax's milk truck. It struck him as odd that it should be where it was, and stationary, but if he hadn't already been alerted he would probably have assumed it had broken down. As it was he started toward it, and the man with his head stuck out of the Navy Building called down as he passed.

"Did it sound like that to you too?"

Usher shrugged and spread his hands, walking on by, his stride just short of urgent. The American voice was very clear in the stillness—and somehow reassuring. They were all Americans in there: Eisenhower had had his offices in the Navy Building during the second half of 1942, so a plaque told the world, and now it served as headquarters of the United States Naval Forces in Europe.

Usher was well short of the truck when he noticed the pools of milk, but he didn't see Eddie Raven's body until he drew level. An extraordinary feeling of disbelief swept him, coupled with a shrinking sensation. The milk was veined with blood, and a slow dripping glug was coming all the time from the back of the truck itself.

The best part of twenty-five years separated Usher from proximity to violence. For a moment his brain seemed to go beyond conscious usefulness, but one long horrified look told him all he needed to know. He was staring at a dead man, freshly dead at that, the eyes not closed yet, the lava-flow of blood still bright and vivid.

"Watch yourself, mister. . . . He's over at Shelley's."

The warning came from the direction of the Roosevelt Memorial. And it scared Usher in a new way; suddenly he felt exposed. Instinctively he crouched behind the truck and, through gaps in its load, searched what he could see of the façade of the hotel he knew so well.

"Some crazy bastard's up there with a gun."

A few more lights were on in the corner building, and a couple of men had emerged onto the American Embassy's front steps, but all they did was increase Usher's sense of isolation. Dawn was giving shape to everything, and the milk was forming a pinkish lake in the gutter. He backed slightly away, sixty-three years old, the onetime soldier in him deciding what was best to do.

Later, whenever he relived those few minutes, he was always surprised at his own agility. More than half the width of the road separated the truck from the hedge that surrounds the gardens in the square. He reached the hedge in six loping strides, half vaulted it, and sank into a deep squat, panting. Ten thudding heartbeats later he moved again, under cover now, grass beneath his feet, the feeling of danger receding with every step but the sense of unreality as stark as before.

"Where are you?" he shouted to whoever had warned him. "Where the hell are you?"

GABRIELLE WILDING said: "There's someone knocking."

"Huh?"

"Someone knocking."

Richard Ireland opened his eyes. "What's the time?"

"About a quarter past five."

"For God's sake," he protested. Then he heard the knocking himself and frowned. More sharply than he realized, he said: "What the hell's going on?"

"There's been some sort of trouble down below."

"Where?"

"I couldn't say. Don't know what woke me up, but something did, and then there was a man bawling his head off in the street. Can't see anything special, though."

The knocking came again—not loud, but urgent and demanding. Gabrielle was standing at the window, not a stitch on, white skin and straw-colored hair. In the lowermost triangle of her vision was a stationary milk truck, small as a child's toy.

"You go," she said.

He managed an early-morning grin. "Why not you?"

"Like this?"

"Give 'em a treat."

"You," she said firmly, returning to the bed.

Ireland pulled on his pajama trousers. "All right, all right," he said, voice raised to placate whoever was there. He was well in control of himself, hardly a trace left over from what had possessed him during the night. The coming daylight helped; that and having company. Yet a memory of himself intruded as he crossed the room.

He turned to check that Gabrielle was covered up. "Why can't they use the house phone?"

"Perhaps we're on fire."

"Very funny."

He bit off a yawn and slid the bolt and opened the door. He opened it a cautious amount, about twelve inches. As he did so he clearly heard Gabrielle gasp. And in the selfsame instant the door was elbowed wide and the man revealed was inside the room with him, coming with a rush, big and bulky.

"Who in the bloody hell—?"

A knee in the groin doubled Ireland over. He recoiled against a heavy chair, a whiff of sweat in his nostrils. Through eyes slitted with pain he saw the door closed with a swift back-heel and watched the man lean hard against it.

"Sit down."

There was a gun in the man's right hand, a rifle, and a narrow black case in the other.

"*Sit down, d'you hear?*"

Ireland obeyed. In a voice that didn't sound like his own any more he faltered: "Is this a joke? . . . Some kind of a joke?"

"Shut up."

Ireland hugged himself, the pain deep in his groin. The man put the case on the floor and moved quickly to the bathroom, glanced inside, then came away. Dark hair, deep-set eyes—Ireland was only just beginning to take him in. Black-and-white-check jacket. Tallish, and broad with it, wide at the shoulders. When he looked at them, he seemed to be memorizing every detail of their faces. He looked at Gabrielle now.

"How long've you got this room?"

"Tonight." She was shaky. "Just for tonight."

"Till noon, you mean?"

She nodded.

"You dressed?"

"No."

"Get dressed, then." The tone was ice-cold, menacing. "You and him both."

Gabrielle risked a question. "What do you want with us?"

37

"You'll find out."

Ireland shot her a frantic look. One side of his mouth was twitching, out of control.

"Try something clever," the man said, "either of you, and you're dead. It's as simple as that."

5:16 A.M.

"SEEMS LIKE he was an old wino, sir. Down and out. Sleeping rough."

That was Dysart. Detective Chief Superintendent McConnell's car was slewed alongside Eagle One by the Upper Brook Street entrance to the American Embassy, their warning flashers blinking in silent syncopation. With them were the Embassy's duty officer and the Marine guard who'd first raised the alert. Out in the road, near the milk truck, Eddie Raven's body remained untouched.

"Thanks, gentlemen," McConnell said, nodding and addressing no one in particular. "Where's the one who was shot at?"

"Over here, sir," Dysart said. "The name's Halifax."

It was fully light now, the sky ribbed with pewter-grey clouds. Halifax wore a white jacket over wash-out jeans, the name of the dairy emblazoned across his back. He smoked nervously, with hardly a pause, and kept on clearing his throat.

McConnell said to him: "D'you know for certain where the shots came from?"

"The second one was from Shelley's."

"Not the first?"

"Couldn't say about that. But the second was from Shelley's for sure. Someone was up on the fire escape."

"Someone?"

"I saw a movement." The hotel was hidden from them, a block away, but he gestured vaguely in its direction. "After the first shot, this was. All I got was a glimpse, but someone was there, all right."

"Which floor?"

"Fourth or fifth."

They could hear the ambulance coming—high low, high low: McConnell hated the sound of the horn, strident with drama. He turned on Dysart and jabbed a finger at the truck.

"No one's going out there while it's possibly still in his field of fire. First thing's to keep the area clear, and that'll mean emergency rerouting."

"I'll get on to Traffic."

"Right away. Any minute there'll be more movement around here than we can cope with."

McConnell had left the Yard with a detective sergeant and a constable, the hairiest driver he had ever known, perhaps the best. With a nod toward Usher he said to the sergeant, "Is that one the night porter?"

"Yes, sir."

"Ask him if he can get us into the hotel under cover."

"Right."

They separated, and he reached into his car for the radio handset. He needed help, and quickly. And there were practical things to be done.

5:20 A.M.

RENATA LANDER heard the ambulance go past the end of Bruton Mews, but only a fraction of her mind took it in. The rest was elsewhere, in a world of its own.

Harry's gun case was gone.

Not only the jacket, not only the money. The gun case too. Five minutes ago she'd noticed. Five minutes ago an impulse took her down to the cupboard in the hall to check whether Harry had come back for his raincoat as well as the jacket.

A measure of relief touched her when she found he hadn't, countered almost at once by the realization that the case was missing.

He always kept it there, always, so there was no point in searching the house. And the only times he took it away were when he went to the rifle club at Lancaster Gate on Thursday evenings.

She had had no sleep since two o'clock. Far too much coffee, far too many cigarettes, and only the cancerous ache of her imagination for company. She went distractedly into the study and pulled back the curtains, all nerves, looking along the cobbled length of the mews. For hours she'd told herself she wouldn't use the telephone, but that was before she knew what she knew now.

Jackman was secretary of the rifle club; Frank Jackman. She got his number from the book and dialed, scrambling a reason together for waking him at such a time.

Burp, burp . . .

She couldn't stop herself, though she'd never met Jackman.

"Hallo."

"Mr. Jackman?"

"Yes."

"Please excuse me for ringing you at such an impossible hour, Mr. Jackman—"

"Who's this speaking?" Gruff and sluggish and aggrieved.

"This is Renata Lander, Mr. Jackman . . . Harry Lander's wife."

"Harry Lander?"

"Yes. Please excuse me, as I say, but I happen to have discovered that Harry's gun case is missing from the house here in Bruton Mews." She listened to herself, the veneer desperately thin. "And since Harry's away for the night—"

"Do you mean the Rauenthaler?"

"He's only got one gun, Mr. Jackman."

"It's been stolen, is that it?"

"I . . . I don't know about that. I was wondering if he had left it at the club."

"Not at the club, Mrs. Lander, no." He cleared his throat. In the background a woman was saying: "Christ Almighty, what a bloody nerve. Have you seen the *time?*" Jackman must have put a hand over the mouthpiece, but a moment later he spoke again. "I'd get on to the police if I were you, Mrs. Lander."

"Yes . . . Yes."

"You can't contact your husband, I suppose?"

"No," she said. "Not until later in the day."

"And you've only just discovered the gun's absence?"

"That's right," she said. Oh God, she thought, oh God—and launched into some stupid lie to account for being up and about with the dawn in the first place. "I really am most sorry to have troubled you, Mr. Jackman."

5:22 A.M.

OUTSIDE, Shelley's is all red brick and white stone.

Usher led McConnell and the sergeant round to the service area at the rear, moving at a jog trot, keeping in the lee of the intervening buildings. There was only one open space to cross—Fairfield Walk—and they took it singly, McConnell waiting until the others were over.

No one was on the fire escape now—he checked as he made his run.

They entered the hotel at one of the delivery bays, dodged through the laundry, and skirted the cold storage. It was a cavernous way in, stone floors and dim lights, quick-thrown echoes as they moved. Somewhere a telephone stopped ringing.

41

"When does this place come alive?"

"Pretty soon," Usher said.

The kitchen was as deserted as everywhere else, cool as a morgue. Usher led them on into the restaurant, slowing to a walk, breathless, McConnell almost alongside.

"How many elevators?"

"Three."

"Staircase?"

"Yes."

"How many ways in and out?"

"Front and back. Plus the fire escape."

"He might not have come into the hotel at all?"

"No."

"Could have used the fire escape merely as a platform?"

"Yes," Usher said. "But I reckon he was in here at one time."

"How d'you know?"

"I don't, not for sure. But I think I heard him—about two hours ago. I heard something, anyway. Someone."

McConnell didn't press him. Now mattered, not two hours ago. No other time but now. They emerged into the foyer, their tread cushioned by a deep pile, and took in what was there—the newsstand and the horseshoe of shops, the staircase spiraling behind the bank of elevators, reception, the glass wall looking onto the street, the immaculate flower tubs, the chandeliers.

"Check the first flight of stairs."

The sergeant went up them three at a time, vanished, then reappeared, shaking his head.

"Stay there," McConnell told him.

A dozen things were racing through his mind. An offensive search was called for, top to bottom. The place was a warren, but he could hardly delay until Special Patrol Group arrived; they might be another fifteen minutes yet.

"How many people in Shelley's right now?"

42

"Hundred and twenty?" Usher suggested. "Hundred and thirty?"

The telephone in the cubicle began to ring. Usher reached it in seconds.

"Night porter."

"At last," a woman complained furiously. "I've rung and rung and got no answer."

"I'm sorry, madam." McConnell was signaling him to damp her down. "I was called away, madam."

"Well, it's most unsatisfactory. There's been a lot of noise up here. First there was a terrible banging, then there was someone on the fire escape near our window, then there was shouting. . . . It's quite monstrous that guests should be subjected to such noise and thoughtlessness. And I'm not the only one, let me say. They've been disturbed in the room next door as well."

"What is your room number, please?"

"237."

"I'll look into the matter, madam, and have the day staff give you an explanation. Meanwhile, you have my apologies."

Usher rang off, steadier than he'd thought possible, the shock and feel of death still unblunted. You read about these things.

McConnell said: "Who's the manager?"

"Mr. Olivares. Roberto Olivares."

"Get him for me—quick." Then, to his sergeant: "And get the crew of Eagle One to join us."

5:30 A.M.

"This is a police message. . . . Attention, this is a police message. If you are living in a building from which Shelley's Hotel is visible, you are warned not to stand near windows or to go outside into the street."

The metallic, amplified voice was vibrant on the stillness.

"We repeat—people who have a view of Shelley's Hotel are warned on no account to stand near windows or to go outside. If anyone disregards this warning, he risks placing himself in extreme danger. . . . As soon as the situation changes you will be notified. Meanwhile, the following are closed to traffic and pedestrians—Grosvenor Square, North Audley Street, Providence Court, Lees Place, Green Street and Fairfield Walk. . . ."

The car cruised by.

"Listen carefully. This is a police message. . . ."

Helen Olivares heard the warning as she listened to McConnell with the other ear. No, she had told him at the start, Mr. Roberto Olivares had toothache and was unobtainable. But she was Mr. Roberto's wife and would he please say what he had to say to her?

This was a minute ago. Now, still cool, she said: "What do you want me to do?"

"Nothing immediately."

"I'll come down."

"Stay where you are. I'm just informing you there is police activity inside the hotel as of now, and as soon as I've got the support I need I'm searching Shelley's floor by floor, room by room. So keep this line open. I may need you."

"You need me now," she said.

Knollenberg's apartment in Green Street offered a partial view of Shelley's topmost floors, and Joan Knollenberg was one of several hundred who heard the police bullhorn; it woke her. This was unusual, because normally she slept through anything—thunder, kids, even Charlie coming home. "Dormouse," he called her.

Almost in surprise, she got up and went at once to the

window, then suddenly realized what she had done and re-treated back into the bedroom.

"Charlie," she said. "Charlie."

She gazed down at his scurf-grey face and wondered what time he'd come in. Kept all hours, Charlie did; and for what? "It's a real drag, honey"—she never gleaned much more than that. Half past five or so, and her Charlie was really exhausted.

From the center of the room she stared out at what she could see of Shelley's and wondered dully what the excitement was about.

5:34 A.M.

THE MAN with the gun kept glancing at Ireland. All the time, his eyes were on the go—here, there, his gaze like a sponge soaking them in, Ireland especially.

"Where've I heard you before?"

Ireland moistened his lips. Heard? *Heard?*

"Where?" the man said. It seemed to matter.

"Television?"

"You an actor?"

"Yes."

How could it matter? They were dressed now, their clothes hurriedly pulled on. The man had rammed the bolt on the door home and dragged a chair into the recess and set it hard against the wall. The girl's brief nakedness hadn't interested him. The room was L-shaped, and from the chair he could watch them constantly. He sat there with the rifle across his thighs, and they sat where he had ordered them to sit—back to back, on either side of the bed.

"Listen," he said. "There's going to be a time when there's speaking to be done on the telephone." He fastened his gaze on Gabrielle. "You'll do it. All of it."

She said nothing.

45

"You'll tell 'em exactly what I tell you—right?"

She nodded.

"No more, no less."

She swallowed and nodded again. "How long's this going to last?"

"Depends."

"On what?"

"Other people."

She wrenched her head away. Sidelong she could see something of Ireland; he was ashen. The man rose from the chair and crossed to the window, a big man, pigeon-toed, like a cat on his feet, the way good squash players were. Now and again Gabrielle glimpsed a sort of bewilderment fleetingly mixed in with the menace. He was sweating thinly.

"At six o'clock," he said, "you'll call room service for coffee."

She said nothing.

"Coffee for two. You and your husband can share."

"He isn't my husband."

Nerves forced it off her tongue, but there was no reaction, no interest.

"Hand me those cigarettes."

A pack of Peter Stuyvesants was beside the bed, and Gabrielle reached for it, nothing else to do but obey, yet wishing to Christ that Ireland didn't make her feel so terribly alone.

5:37 A.M.

HELEN OLIVARES rode down to the ground floor in the fast elevator. The curlers were still in her hair, but she had thrown on slacks and a blouse and scrawled a note for Roberto. *Stay where you are*, she'd written. *Don't answer the door without calling switchboard first. H.*

The elevator doors opened with a soft whirr, and she stepped into the foyer.

"Hold it!"

She spun round. With a squirm of alarm she saw the sergeant on the stairs with a pistol pointed at her. In the same instant, on the fringes of her vision, she was aware of another man.

"Who are you?" this one snapped.

She recognized the voice. "I'm Helen Olivares. I was speaking to you on the phone."

"You were told to stay put."

"The switchboard needs manning."

"Your night porter's here."

"My husband and I are responsible to our guests, and if you're about to conduct a room-to-room search it's my duty to inform them personally."

"Very well," McConnell conceded. No harm in that. God, what a lady, though.

Yorke and Dysart had arrived, and the minutes were ticking by. He was still too thin on the ground, but a start had to be made. Dysart he ordered to check the fire escape. Yorke and the sergeant—the only one among them who was armed—he sent to the fifth floor with instructions to work along its length.

Helen Olivares hurried to reception, where she opened a drawer. "They should have a list of names."

Yorke and the sergeant weren't waiting for anything like that. The elevator doors sealed them in, and the indicator light blinked off.

McConnell said tersely: "We aren't on a social visit, Mrs. Olivares. Start warning the fifth floor what to expect, but first of all put me on to New Scotland Yard."

5:42 A.M.

In the elevator Yorke cocked an eye at the sergeant and said: "What d'you reckon?"

47

"Going through the motions, if you ask me."

"Think so?"

"What sort of madman looses off at someone and then stays put?"

Yorke half shrugged. "What sort of madman looses off in the first place?"

5:43 A.M.

WHEN THE phone buzzed, the three of them in the room stiffened slightly. It buzzed twice before the man with the gun jerked his head at Gabrielle.

"Take it." He changed his grip on the rifle.

She slid along the bed and lifted the phone off the hook.

"Room 501?" Helen Olivares began. "Good morning. The management offers sincere apologies for calling you at this hour, but there has been an unfortunate incident in the street nearby and the police find it necessary to make an immediate search of Shelley's . . . Hallo? Hallo?"

"Yes," Gabrielle said. "I'm here."

"You will probably find the police will be calling at 501 within the next few minutes. It will be appreciated if you give them every assistance. We can assure you they will keep their disturbance of you to the minimum."

Already, on only her second call, she had found a pattern of words. The line went dead, and Gabrielle hung up, her pulse accelerating.

"Who was it?" the man said.

"Manager's office."

Some of it must have carried; ten feet, that's all he was away. Yet he stared at her as if he hadn't heard, and the demand of his stare was fiercer than any question.

"The police are making a room-to-room check."

He jerked to his feet as if a spring was in him.

"Now," she heard herself say.

He used the rifle as a pointer, jabbing. "In there," he snapped at Ireland. "In there." The bathroom. "There—and hurry."

Ireland was nowhere fast enough. The man swore and swung the butt. "Move, d'you hear?" Then he grabbed Gabrielle by the arm and wrenched her round to face him.

"Listen." He felt like iron. There was a wildness in his eyes, and her insides shrank from it. "Listen to me. The two of us'll be in there, and unless you play along, he'll take the consequences. . . . Got that?"

Gabrielle nodded, on tiptoe from the grip on her arm. But he wasn't satisfied she understood.

"There's a dead man in the street. I've got nothing to lose."

In a whisper she managed: "What do I do?"

"Send 'em away. Keep them out."

The sound of rapping cut him off. Along the corridor. The three of them stood as still as stone. The rapping stopped, and there were muffled voices and then there was silence again.

"When they come," the man said, "you don't let 'em in. Nothing's wrong here. *Nothing*, understand? Tell 'em everything's okay."

"Yes."

He let go of her and went into the bathroom. The door was left slightly ajar, and she heard him speak to Ireland—though what he said she didn't catch, and it didn't matter. Everything else could take care of itself. She felt numb. And frightened in a new way. Trembling, she reached for a cigarette and lit it, blowing smoke.

A small fraction of the morning went by, with her mind in desperation over what must somehow not be allowed to happen.

Nothing's wrong here. Tell 'em that. Everything's okay. . . .

———

49

It seemed a nightmare length of time before they came. And she started when she heard them. Straining for them though she'd been, for a long moment she seemed quite unable to move, locked in a terrible hesitancy.

"Open up, please. . . . Police."

She reached the door and slid back the bolt. First she saw Yorke, then the sergeant, only a fraction of a second between, and, with heightened awareness, she thought how ordinary the sergeant looked, like a clerk, a rust-red sweater beneath his jacket.

Yorke said: "Sorry to bother you, but we're making a check along this floor. Have you been disturbed in any way?"

"No."

"Heard anything unusual?"

"No," she said.

"Are you alone here?"

"No."

He was looking past her at the rumpled bed. Got it, his eyes flickered, misreading her indecision. Then they came back to her, and he nodded and sort of smiled, at which point she thought everything was going to be all right. But to her dismay he took a step forward.

"If you'll excuse me, we'll just take a look."

"No." It came with a rush. "You can't do that. . . ."

"We won't be a minute."

Frantic now. "No," she said. She stood in his way, beside herself, beginning to bluster, committed to reasons for their not coming in that weren't reasons at all, and aware as she gestured and tried to hold her ground that she was quickening their interest with every passing moment.

"Sorry, miss," Yorke said. "But we've orders to inspect each room."

On the very limit of her vision on her right she saw the bathroom door begin to swing open.

"No!" she cried then, not to Yorke any more, turning sharply as she did so with her arms uplifted.

The shot almost deafened her. Yorke clutched himself and staggered backward, falling, spinning sideways. She had a vivid impression of the one in the sweater flinching and dropping into a crouch, his right hand coming up. Then the door was booted to and slammed violently shut, and the man with the rifle was flat against the wall.

Outside, they could hear groaning, shuffling, dragging. Inside, there was an appalled silence, five or six seconds of it before the scream came.

"What have you done? . . . *What have you done?*"

Gabrielle retreated, a phrase from her childhood resurrecting.

"Mother of God—"

In the bathroom Ireland had started being sick.

DAYLIGHT

5:48 A.M.

THE SERGEANT got his hands under Yorke's armpits and began to drag him like a sack. Doors were opening all along the corridor, and startled faces showed themselves.

"Get inside!"

He was moving backward, eyes never leaving 501, the pistol still drawn. A man in crumpled white pajamas came out of a room and tried to help by grabbing hold of Yorke's legs, but the sergeant yelled at him.

"Go 'way!" Then: "Call the elevator."

"Is he dead?"

"Call the elevator!"

The man vanished behind him. Yorke moaned, limp as a straw doll. A smear of blood was on the carpet, and the sergeant's hands were warm and sticky. Yorke's cap lay upside down like something put out by a beggar. The blood began where the cap was, and the carpet was soaking it up.

"Oh my Christ," an appalled woman wailed from a doorway. "What's been—?"

"Get back in! Get in and keep in!"

The sergeant had reached the top of the stairs. The man in white pajamas was still around.

"It's coming. . . . Coming."

He was bald and potbellied and had a mouth like Ernest Borgnine; incredibly, this registered. A sound like a gulp came from the elevator shaft, and the sergeant heard the doors hum open. His eyes were still fixed on 501. But for the girl, he'd have got off a shot. Quicker than blinking there'd been a chance—but for the girl.

"Now take his legs. *Now.*"

They lugged Yorke inside, and the man hit the ground-floor button with the flat of his hand. The doors slid together, and they started moving. Yorke was losing no end of blood, but an ambulance was close, thank God.

"Who did it?"

The sergeant made no reply. He was looking at Yorke's face and didn't seem to be listening.

"Which room number was it?" the man in pajamas said. "I'm 508." It could only have been nerves. "My wife and I checked in last night."

Their knees sagged as the descent ended. The doors opened. McConnell was there, McConnell and others, close, more hatless men scattered across the foyer: Special Patrol Group had arrived.

"Where is he?"

"501. End room but one. Holed up with a girl."

"See him?"

"Not properly."

Somebody must have rung down. Yorke was lifted out of the sergeant's care and hurried away. He saw the blood on his hands now and started to wipe them, reaction setting in. The man in pajamas seemed unaware that he was surrounded by police, and he launched into a preliminary version of what had happened, very excited with his gestures.

"Save it, will you?" he was told. Someone said: "Thanks for your help." Then someone else shouldered up to him, someone with a pocket tape recorder. "I'm Kent," this someone said. "Kent of the *Star*"—and he was in his element.

Special Patrol Group consists of an inspector, two sergeants, and forty policemen—all armed. They had come in closed vans and had arrived at Shelley's thirty-six minutes exactly after McConnell said he wanted them. McConnell nodded to his own sergeant and turned urgently toward Inspector Savage.

"First thing's to clear the floor, Bunny. Everybody out."

"Right."

"The people in 500 to be brought down by way of the fire escape. That's the room at the very end. Everyone else, from 502 upwards, to use the stairs and elevators."

"Right." Savage had a lean, marathon-runner's build and sported a narrow bootlace mustache which always seemed to McConnell at least a decade out of fashion.

"Give them maximum possible cover. Once 501's satisfactorily quarantined we'll go into the question of how and where you're best deployed." McConnell's tone was crisp and matter-of-fact. "Looks as though we could have a siege situation on our hands."

Savage swung away, already giving orders. McConnell crossed to the switchboard at the side of reception and spoke to Helen Olivares: the curlers were still in her hair.

"Who's in 501?"

"Richard Ireland and a Gabrielle Wilding." Deadpan: this was the way the world was now.

"Ireland?" Surprise was a luxury he rarely allowed himself. "Richard Ireland the actor?"

"Yes."

He pursed his lips. Ireland? First a random wino in the square, and then a uniformed constable?

"Get him for me."

She hesitated.

"Call 501."

He glanced across the foyer. One elevator had already gone up, another was loading.

"501 doesn't answer," Helen Olivares said.

"Try again." McConnell waited, remembering how awful Yorke had looked. Unconsciously he fingered his black tie. Not again, surely not again?

Helen Olivares said suddenly: "A moment, please."

She used her head to indicate the telephone he should go to. He snatched it up. "Who's there?" he asked.

"This is Gabrielle Wilding." Terrified, close to a whisper.

"I'm a police officer, Miss Wilding, and I want to speak to Richard Ireland."

"You have to speak to me."

He ignored that. "Richard Ireland, please."

An erratic sibilance ran along the line. Either she was waiting for him to say something more or she was being given instructions; he couldn't decide. It wasn't until she spoke again that he realized the delay might have been due to her searching for a choice of words.

In the same shaky whisper as before, she said: "Richard Ireland's not able to speak."

McConnell was quick to read the clue. "How many of you in that room?"

No reply.

"Two? Or three?"

He waited, sensitive to the dreadful realities of her position. "Listen—"

The line went dead. Three, he decided. Right or wrong, he guessed three.

5:55 A.M.

DYSART had found an ejected shell case on the second level of the fire escape at the very instant that Yorke was shot. Not certain where to climb to, he'd made an entry at each of the floors above him, reaching the fifth only seconds after Yorke was humped into the elevator.

The sight of the blood trail and the police cap had sent him thudding frantically down the escape, and he'd arrived in time to help carry Yorke to the waiting ambulance.

"Eagle One calling Alpha Control . . ."

He sweated, at the car now, distress and anger in his voice as he reported to Division. One of the nicest youngsters he'd ever worked with, Yorke was.

"Go ahead, Eagle One."

"Constable Yorke's been wounded at Shelley's Hotel and is at present on his way by ambulance to St. George's Hospital. Am closing down temporarily until I've reported back to Chief Superintendent McConnell. Special Patrol Group is at the scene, so it's their war now."

"How bad's Peter Yorke?"

"It didn't look good to me. In the chest, I'd say. . . . Over and out."

He returned to Shelley's—left and right and right again. There were barriers across Lees Place and Upper Brook Street, and police motorcyclists were on the prowl, their radios chattering. A lone woman was being shepherded down the fire escape by an armed detective humping some luggage. Some of Shelley's day-shift staff were bunched together around the delivery bays and by the storage areas and in the outer kitchen. Passing, he heard: "Room service the same as usual— 'cept for the fifth. Same as usual, yes. I know, brother, but that's what she says. . . ."

Dysart moved on through to the foyer, to where McConnell

56

was briefing a scene-of-crime squad on the removal of Eddie Raven's body.

McConnell finished: "Now we know where the gunman is, there's no risk, so you're okay for photographs and a locality search. Take your time."

Dysart came up, the ejected shell case held between his fingers. "Found this on the fire escape, sir, between the second and third flights."

McConnell took it from him. *Who* concerned him, rather than *how,* and *what with.* In a few minutes more the fifth floor would be cleared: already the elevators were disgorging the first evacuees.

"Only the one?"

"I wasn't making a special search, and when Constable Yorke was shot, I quit to help him."

"It's quite light." The ballistics people were the ones who'd be interested. "The others probably drifted. We'll get them."

"Yes, sir."

Helen Olivares called from the switchboard. "The Assistant Commissioner wants you."

"Right away." McConnell paused before reaching for the telephone, his thoughts fragmented. A proper headquarters was necessary, radio as well as other links. He'd never run the show from here. "Nothing else?" he asked Dysart, raising the shell case shoulder high.

"No, sir," Dysart said. But then he fumbled in a pocket. The bitter hurt of Yorke's disaster had rattled him. "Sorry, there was this as well."

McConnell glanced abstractedly at what Dysart gave him— a luggage tag, plastic-covered, its fastener snapped off. On the tag was printed H. R. LANDER, 14 BRUTON MEWS, LONDON, W.1.

6:00 A.M.

ROBERTO OLIVARES woke to a pain like a broken jaw deep in the left side of his face.

"Helen?" He squinted blearily at where she usually was at such a time. "Helen?"

He propped himself on an elbow, the balm of the Bacardi all worn away.

Ayeeee ... "Helen?"

Just then he saw the note standing against the bedside clock. With a grunt he picked it up. Don't answer the door without calling the switchboard first? A fine time for mysteries, he thought indignantly, but obeyed the instruction.

"What you doing on the switchboard?" He'd gone half an octave higher than normal. Helen told him, and he didn't believe her. "You're crazy. . . . In Shelley's? Right now, here in Shelley's?"

"Right now," she said, "in 501. The whole of the floor's evacuated, and the police—"

"Where to, evacuated?"

"Writing room and TV lounge and—"

"Jesus," Roberto said.

"Get dressed and come on down."

"Sure."

Gingerly he probed with his tongue, forced to side-step the hope that none of this was real. And a sudden memory made him shout at his so-cool wife four floors below.

"What about that Jupiter rubbish you told me in the night? An uneventful day tomorrow, and God knows what—remember?" With less heat, he followed up: "This shooting, this man with a gun . . ."

But already she wasn't there.

6:11 A.M.

THE NURSE in Casualty syringed Yorke's blood sample into the standard bottle, sealed it tight, and disappeared at a run, the doors flapping behind her.

"Watch the oxygen," the duty doctor growled to others in the glossy white-painted room, "and for Christ's sake hook that bottle higher."

He slid the long needle into the vein in Yorke's left arm and began to bind it steady.

"Okay." He nodded, and a second nurse adjusted the clip on the saline-glucose drip.

Yorke's face had a waxy look. He was lying on his left side, stripped naked from the waist up. A thin froth of blood was on his lips. The bullet had drilled into his chest about three inches below his right collarbone, and the gaping exit wound was haemorrhaging badly.

The doctor gently thumbed down the lid of one of Yorke's eyes. "Sister."

"Yes, doctor."

"Tell the ward to come and collect—and tell 'em to make it fast." His tone changed slightly as he went on looking at Yorke. "God, they *do* get younger, don't they?"

"Who?"

"The police, luv, the police."

6:14 A.M.

McCONNELL stood with Savage in the angle of wall where the stairs led down from the fifth floor. Three of Savage's armed plain-clothes men covered the corridor; every room but one was empty now.

McConnell lifted the bullhorn to his mouth. "My name is McConnell," he began, working by the book, "and I'm a police officer. I am speaking to one of the occupants in 501. I am speaking to the person in 501 who is armed." He paused and licked his lips. "The hotel is completely surrounded. My suggestion to you is that you come out of the room with your hands raised above your head. There will be no shooting if you do this. Leave the rifle behind and come out with your hands raised."

With a sense of futility he paused again. Every word was a step in the dark, and he wished to God he knew who he was dealing with. Not Ireland, no; he was reasonably sure of that. But no matter who it was, there were absolutely no pressures he could apply. Savage could fret for action as much as he liked, but time was their only worth-while weapon. Threats were useless and could misfire. Time and patience and steady nerves—they'd need all three. Yet at moments like these the waiting game seemed like a partial defeat.

"Listen to me," he tried, no more than a trace of command in his voice. "Let the girl go. Open the door and let her out. What d'you want with two people in there? One's enough. One's all you need. Let the girl go, whoever you are. . . ."

Noel Lander had no recollection of the dream, any dream, no thoughts at all worth speaking of except for the dawning realization that he was into another day; and that breakfast would follow a shower and that school would follow breakfast.

He surveyed the posters at the foot of his bed through eyes bleary with sleep—the earth like a beautiful blue-and-white marble suspended in darkness, and the arrowhead formation of geese in flight across a sunset marshland. On another wall a streamer announced THIS IS ABROAD. HOME IS SOMEWHERE ELSE.

The posters were fairly new, but the streamer dated back a couple of years, to the time they were all in Ankara. Jimmy Baatz had sent it over from Columbus, Ohio, which is where home really was—or used to be. Jimmy Baatz would just about be shaving now, Noel decided, which struck him as a pretty incredible opening thought for any morning, rain or shine. He stayed with Jimmy for a while, remembering the time he had cut his eyelashes off because someone had said how long and attractive they were. Nut . . . Others from Columbus had a place in his reverie, but mainly he was occupied with Jimmy and how it had been when they were together.

Different. No better, no worse. Just different . . . Perhaps better, if he properly gave his mind to it. For one thing, his mother and father didn't row so much in those days.

Howard Kent's eyes were small and black and eager for drama. Not merely at the obvious times, such as now, but always. Even over a drink with a colleague in Fleet Street's Wig and Pen the door never opened without Kent showing a glint of hopeful anticipation that a story was about to be born, something he could dig into and go deep. And do it first, ahead of the others, sod everyone along the way.

"I understand you're the manager at Shelley's, Mr. Olivares?"

"Correct, yes."

"And the shooting—the shooting of the man in Grosvenor Square, that is—took place from the outside fire escape?"

"I believe, yes."

"Did you hear the shots yourself?"

"My wife did."

"At what time?"

"Ask her, please. I have a bad toothache and I cannot tell you when they were."

"How many shots were fired?"

"Ask my wife, please."

Of course. Kent's eyes glinted. You bet.

"Perhaps you *can* tell me," he said, continuing to crowd Olivares as he moved across the foyer, "who Gabrielle Wilding is?"

"How should I know a thing like that?"

"Because she's the girl in 501 with Richard Ireland, and I thought—"

"I don't know," Olivares snapped, "and I don't care."

Kent raked him with a wicked glance. "It's your hotel, Mr. Olivares."

"And the guests in it have lives of their own. . . . Now leave me, please." He screwed his face and felt his jaw, as if pain were something exclusive to himself, waving Kent away. "I have enough trouble without you."

6:17 A.M.

"SHUT HIM UP," the man with the rifle demanded suddenly. A vein bulged in his forehead like a worm beneath the skin. "Shut that bastard up out there."

McConnell's voice brayed at them through the bullhorn, seeming to come from just beyond the door, loud and inescapable. Gabrielle Wilding hesitated, watching the gun and where it was pointed.

"Use the phone, for Christ's sake. Tell 'em to stop that noise."

She went to the telephone and spoke to Helen Olivares. "Hold it away from your head," the man warned her. "If they've any messages, I want to hear them. Nothing's private any more—got that?"

He looked at her wildly, with the same unnerving stare. Richard Ireland sat at the end of the bed, sweat on his upper lip like beads. He couldn't keep his fingers still, but the rest of him seemed turned to stone.

"Quit now," McConnell persisted, breaking a seconds-long wait. "You will have to quit in the end, so why not now? Come out of there with your hands raised above—"

The man swore and put a shot into the bathroom, firing from the hip, teeth clenched and cords stretched in his neck.

The girl stiffened, flinching, and Ireland jerked to his feet to the smash of glass. Outside and inside there was silence, shock and apprehension pounding every heartbeat, time somehow turned back on itself.

With her gaze locked in alarm on the detective monitoring the call, Helen Olivares started saying frantically: "Hallo, hallo . . . Hallo . . ."

"We're all right," the girl replied. She was trembling, the acrid stink of cordite flaring her nostrils. "We're all right."

"Sure?"

"He wants the one who's using the bullhorn to cut it out." An enormous effort was required. "He wants it stopped, d'you hear? . . . *Please,*" she begged.

Downstairs the sergeant nodded and sent a constable sprinting to the elevator. In the room the girl did as she was told and covered the mouthpiece and listened. Along the corridor McConnell conferred urgently with Savage.

Then the girl came back to Helen Olivares. "Next time, he says, next time he won't just waste the shot."

"The message is on its way." How calm she managed to sound. "Believe me when I say we're doing everything we can to help. . . . Try and tell him that, will you?"

The man stepped close and cut them off. The girl moved away from him uncertainly, stiffly, not knowing where he expected her to go. He backed across the room to the windows and looked out, standing by the wall, poking the curtain aside with the muzzle of the rifle. The room faced east. North Audley Street was below, Oxford Street to the left, Grosvenor Square to the right, but nothing except North Audley Street was to be seen, empty now, as quiet as if the plague had struck. Only amid the jumble of rooftops opposite was there any sign of life—two men, crouched behind cover, one signaling the other.

"Close these curtains."

No one moved.

"You." The man motioned to Ireland. "Are you deaf?"

He switched on some lights as the room darkened. All the time they were watching what he did and he was watching them, the tension like a living thing. Time and chance had brought them together, but the nightmare was part of something else; it had to be.

Ireland found his tongue at last. "Who are you?"

"Don't push your luck."

"You can't keep us here forever."

"Give me one good reason."

Ireland dropped his gaze, no match for the glare that nailed him, broken and hollowed out already.

"Give me one good reason, I said."

Ireland shook his head. His eyes met Gabrielle Wilding's and shied from the flicker of contempt that greeted him. The man crossed the room and stood close to the door with his head cocked. Perhaps he'd heard something. Then he stepped back and to one side. He spoke to the girl this time, the same uncanny strangeness about the way he looked at her, as if they'd never met.

"Have the coffee sent up now," he said. "Tell 'em to leave it ten feet from the door."

Gabrielle Wilding nodded fearfully, just short of terror, a tiny part of her mind fleetingly preoccupied with a thought about her mother; she'd know soon, perhaps knew already.

"Black coffee." The man was never still. "And a dozen packets of breakfast cereal. Corn flakes, crispies. Big ones, family packs." She frowned, and he snorted as if it amused him, making her skin crawl.

6:29 A.M.

FIVE HOURS' sleep was plenty for Mulholland; not since he was a boy, still growing, had he really needed more. Now, in the moment of waking, he reached as usual for the radio and switched it on. Mary Kay used to rib him about the time he woke in mid-Atlantic on a 747 and started a groping exploration of the thighs of a woman in the next seat. But habit died hard, and Ralph Mulholland was a creature of habit. "What's more," Mary Kay had since got around to adding, "the lady rather liked it, dammit."

Mulholland rolled onto his side and listened without really listening to the coda of an up-tempo version of "Moon River" —fine, he supposed, if you liked that kind of thing, which he didn't. The music ended and silence took its place, brief but intense, and he thanked God that Winfield House was spared the dyspeptic murmur of London's traffic even at the peak of times. Now, coming up to six-thirty precisely, it was country quiet, and a stranger to the house would hardly have believed the Embassy was less than a ten-minute urban drive away.

Unless, that is, someone like Grattan drove you. All hell could happen then, and usually it did. You never knew for sure where you would end up with Grattan.

The prenews jingle ended and the headlines began. China had exploded her most powerful nuclear device yet, Spain had devalued the peseta, a Chilean aircraft had crashed in the Atacama Desert, with the loss of seventy-four lives.

"An unknown man was shot dead in London's Grosvenor Square early this morning, and, shortly afterwards, a policeman was wounded in Shelley's Hotel nearby. The police have surrounded the hotel, where a gunman is holding two people hostage. . . ."

Mulholland raised a broad eyebrow. He picked up the telephone and turned the radio down. Ten seconds later he was in contact with the duty officer at the Embassy.

"I've just heard the six-thirty news, BBC. Tell me what happened." He listened for a while, then cut in. "None of our people is in any way involved?"

"No, sir."

"That's all I want to know."

"A lot of streets in the vicinity are blocked off right now, Mr. Ambassador, so you may have to come in by a different route. In case the situation's unchanged, I suggest you take Upper Grosvenor Street."

"Thank you," Mulholland said. "We'll check nearer the time."

6:42 A.M.

RENATA LANDER lay asleep on the sitting room's chintz-covered couch, curled up there like a child, and Noel stood in the doorway at the foot of the stairs thinking how exhausted she looked. The ashtray she'd used was piled with a heap of stubs and the coffee cup was empty. Everywhere the lights were on, and the air was stale and dry from smoke.

Unease touched him when he saw his mother, a sort of despair as he tried to fathom the mysteries of love and rage and pain. He made a small sound as he started to withdraw, enough to wake her.

"Noel?" She sat up abruptly, a strand of dark hair across her face. "What time is it?"

"Nearly seven, I guess."

She seemed to hesitate, as if dreading the answer. "Is your father home?"

"No," he said, and her eyes went dead, something draining away.

They were moving Eddie Raven's body. The photographs had all been taken and the area minutely examined. Now Halifax could remove the milk truck, and they could hose the gutters clean and sweep the broken glass away.

"Poor old sod," the doctor said to the scene-of-crime sergeant.

"Never knew what hit him."

The ambulance men lifted the stretcher. Despite the bulk of his wrappings, Eddie Raven didn't weigh all that much. And even in death there was about him the smell of total defeat.

6:44 A.M.

THE TELEPHONE buzzed in 501, and Gabrielle Wilding was ordered to answer it.

"Yes?"

"The packets of cereal have been delivered." Helen Olivares. "Also the coffee."

She obeyed the signal and hung up, sick in the stomach, nerves like singing wires.

"Listen to me," the man said. "First thing you'll do is open the door. You, yes. Second thing is you'll bring the coffee in."

She nodded.

"There's something else. After that you're going to open each of those packets and scatter the stuff to either side along the corridor. Make a carpet of it. If anybody starts coming anywhere near this room I want to hear them before they arrive."

She nodded again.

"God help your friend if you decide to make a run." He paused, confident he had her on a string. "You could, you know. There'll be nothing to stop you."

She stared, her gaze wavering, lips apart. He looked quite mad.

"You could, but you won't." He motioned to Ireland. "Tell her you expect her to come back in."

67

Ireland seemed to have lost his tongue.

"*Tell her!*"

Ireland swallowed. In a flat voice he said: "Come back."

"Again."

Humiliation used to be a word. Fear belonged in scripts. "Come back," he said to her.

The man positioned himself behind Ireland, addressing the girl. "When I tell you to open the door, do it fast. Pull it wide and stand there. Count up to five, then step outside. And think about your friend and me."

He worked the rifle's mechanism, metal on metal, *snap snap*. Gabrielle Wilding moved to the door and slid the bolt across, as quiet as a conspirator. A handful of seconds elapsed.

"Now."

She yanked the door open and stood without moving. The quiet in the corridor was the quiet of people holding their breath. Then Gabrielle Wilding sucked in hers and walked out of the room. The tray and the packets of cereal she saw immediately, about four paces to the left. All the doors along the corridor were open, giving the walls a strangely broken appearance. A narrow slice of a man's face and shoulders protruded from one of the gaps, and, where the stairs led down beside the elevator, somebody else was partially visible—bootlace mustache, florid complexion, about a sixth of him showing. The nearer of the two was five rooms away, and he shrank back when she emerged, then exposed himself a little more and encouraged her to go toward him, signaling with the pistol she saw in his hand.

No word, no sound at all, only the urgent dumb show.

She walked as far as where the tray of coffee was. From the room they couldn't see her now. She stopped at the tray and looked down the corridor, shook her head, spread her hands.

Come *on*, the man in the doorway mouthed, showing himself even more, empty holster on one hip.

No. She shook her head again, face screwed, making small frantic chopping motions. No . . . *No.*

She bent and picked up the tray. When she faced about she saw a third man at the fire-escape end of the corridor. He was crouching, red extinguishers and buckets of sand in the recess where he had positioned himself.

She went back into 501, the coffee slopping, the sense of unreality and a terrible awareness schizophrenically combined. There were three cups, she noticed; three cups, biscuits, cream, sugar. Ireland was where she had last seen him; the man too. The man jerked the rifle, and she put the tray down, trembling violently.

His eyes seemed to glitter as she passed him on the way out again. She didn't so much as glance at Ireland, though her feeling was that he was looking at her. Momentarily everything seemed too far away, but as she emerged into the corridor a second time the sense of distortion passed.

The men she had seen before were still there, still in the same places, watching her now, no signals, no mime. She opened the first of the packets and showered the contents across the width of the corridor. Then she retreated a little, bringing the remainder with her, tearing another open. A patchy scatter of corn flakes began to cover the carpet. With hindsight, with cunning, with calculated coolness, she might have left a path where a person could walk unheard. But none of these things were hers, and she did what she'd been told to do because compliance somehow seemed to offer the best chance of survival.

Questions were there all the time, beating tiny fists against her senses. Why them? . . . And who was he? . . . And what would happen?

She emptied the packets on both sides of 501, starting several paces from the door, throwing each packet down as she finished with it. She didn't once lift her eyes to those who watched; their impotence heightened her own. She tossed the last packet away and backed into the room. Without being ordered to, she closed the door and slid the bolt across.

"Fine," the man said, as if she were his ally. "Fine."

She went to the bed, everything gone green, and glared at Ireland. D'you know what you owe me? her mind stormed. D'you realize what I've done for you?

Inspector Savage, in the angle of wall by the elevator, made a spitting sound as soon as the door was shut. The armed policeman framed by 509 turned and shrugged.

"He's got her on wheels."

Savage nodded.

"What next?" the policeman said, voice right down.

"Wait and see, that's next. Wait a week if need be."

"Drink the coffee," the man said, nodding at them both. "You first."

He watched them. He didn't tell them which cups to use.

"Drink it all."

Minutes later he was still watching, eyes knowing and suspicious, and the third cup remained untouched.

6:59 A.M.

IN POLICE REPORTS and inventories the caravan was referred to as a "mobile incident post," but McConnell would have none of that.

"Headquarters established in Blackburne's Mews," he reported to Control Room at New Scotland Yard. "I am immediately behind the American Embassy at the junction with Upper Brook Street. The situation in Shelley's remains unchanged, with SPG in position under Inspector Savage. Outside, the affected area is cordoned off and no-go to traffic and pedestrians. Inside, the fifth floor has been cleared except for the gunman and his two hostages."

In the caravan with him were his assigned deputy, Superintendent Llewellyn, a radio operator, and an inspector responsible for press liaison. There wasn't much room, and the inspector had his hands full with television and newspaper reporters seeking details, permissions, favors. Parked close by in the mews were half a dozen patrol cars and a dog handlers' van. The scene-of-crime squad was present as well, at a loose end now that Eddie Raven had gone to the mortuary, and a couple of sergeants seconded from Division were on stand-by call.

"If only we knew who the hell he is, we'd have something to work on," McConnell complained. "Not knowing's a bastard. Using the hailer at him's a waste of time. Might as well sound off at a wall."

Llewellyn agreed, Llewellyn who wasn't renowned as the most cautious of men.

"I don't see that we've got any short cuts," McConnell said, studying the sketch Llewellyn had had made of the fifth floor's layout and Special Patrol Group's dispositions. "He's contained, which is something, but that's about all. There isn't anything to use against him at the moment, not a blind thing." He rubbed his eyes. "He's got it made, the way things are. Food and drink for the asking. Sanitation . . . He can really call the kind of tune he chooses."

"Eventually he'll have to sleep."

"He could put the two of them out of action first—gag them, tie them up. We're still at square one even if he does go under for a while. They're at risk the moment we make a move, and the more scared we make him the more trigger-happy he's going to be."

McConnell bit on a peppermint. Seven o'clock and they'd as good as reached stalemate.

"If only we knew what he *wants*," he muttered, voicing his thoughts. "If only we had a reason *why*."

"And a name."

He nodded. "That's the key. Answer that one and we can maybe find a weapon to tackle him with. . . . All we have so far's this report from one of the guests that he was disturbed during the night and saw a man in his corridor wearing a black-and-white-check jacket and carrying a case. Six-footer, seen from the back, dark-haired. Before any shots were fired, this was. . . . That's our sum total. Otherwise we're groping in the dark." He paused. "Any follow-up yet on that luggage tag?"

7:04 A.M.

THE NUMBER was not listed, but there were ways around that.

"Mrs. Ireland?"

"Speaking."

"My name is Kent, Mrs. Ireland." She was a hundred miles away, near Poole. "Howard Kent, of the London *Star*."

"Oh, yes?"

"I wondered if you can tell me something of your thoughts and feelings about your husband at this time?"

"I don't understand what you mean. And isn't it a little early?"

It hadn't occurred to him that she might not have heard. It didn't seem possible. The radio, friends . . . neighbors. *He*'d known for an hour, a whole hour. "Don't you know what's happened, Mrs. Ireland?"

"No, I do not." She sounded tired. "What exactly's this about?"

He explained, unable to believe his luck, an opening paragraph in his mind already. Mr. Ice-cool's wife . . . Mr. Smooth-as-Glass. At first she didn't believe him, but her tone soon changed. "Oh my God," she began to say, punctuating every sentence he brought together with "oh my God." But this didn't last for long, and soon he was putting words into her mouth, something he could quote.

"This must have come as a terrible shock to you, Mrs. Ireland. . . . In a crisis like this you'd expect something very much in character from him, wouldn't you, Mrs. Ireland? . . . You'll want to be in London as soon as possible, I presume, Mrs. Ireland? . . ."

"Yes . . . Yes." Confused, she answered him. "But what was he doing at Shelley's?"

Damned if he was telling her that. So far and no further. "I couldn't say, Mrs. Ireland."

"Normally he stays at the Churchill."

She started coming back at him then, shock pumping the questions out of her.

"I'd call Scotland Yard if I were you, Mrs. Ireland. Check with them for an up-to-the-minute report, and insist that you be kept in constant touch."

Always leave them indebted to you.

"They'll be all right, you'll see. They'll come to no harm."

He could have kicked himself.

" 'They'?" she queried, quick as a flash. "What do you mean—'they'?"

The man drained his cup, the coffee gone cold now, and shifted his gaze from Ireland to the girl.

"Know what I want?"

He was the length of the bed away, sitting on a chair with its straight wooden back between his legs, the gun across his thighs.

"Know what I want out of this?"

They waited, unable to decipher him, not trusting the abrupt change of mood. The edges of the curtains were frayed with the glare of the day outside, but the only world for them was here, enclosed and deadly.

"You ever heard of compensation?"

"Yes."

"Know what it means?"

"Yes."

"That's what I want," he announced. He blinked at them both as if baffled by a memory. "Compensation . . . Recompense. That's what I'm entitled to, that's what I'm going to get. Believe you me."

7:12 A.M.

ROBERTO OLIVARES surveyed the shambles that had been made of the writing room and groaned. Around forty people had taken possession of the place, some dressed, some still in their night attire, no one shaved, no one washed, some in chairs, some on the floor. And all without exception surly.

"Good morning again, ladies and gentlemen." He produced a pain-racked distortion of the Olivares smile. "Once more I have to apologize for the situation and the inconvenience. But now I am happy to tell you that we have facilities available to you. Rooms 107, 108, 109, and 110 are yours to use. All on the first floor." He stood with his hands clasped like a priest, lips bravely back over his teeth. "All I would be asking, ladies and gentlemen, is that you are as prompt as possible when you take your turn."

He swung on his heel, and the trained expression died as if he had pulled a switch. He marched into the foyer and went round reception to where the switchboard was. His wife flashed him a glance, brisk as could be, calls coming all the time.

She said: "We're going to have to manage without most of the day staff."

74

"Impossible."

"The area's cordoned off, so how do they get past the barriers? Some I could name will be too scared even to try."

"What're we going to do?" He spread his hands.

"Manage—what else? . . . Hallo, yes, this is Shelley's."

Roberto Olivares leaned against the switchboard console. "I've got to get over to Gilbert, Helen. At nine sharp I've got to have this toothache seen to."

"If you go, you may not get back."

"Otherwise I start to scream."

Of all days. "Hallo, yes? . . . One moment, please." Of all days, she thought.

7:15 A.M.

"Mrs. Lander?" the detective sergeant said.

"That's right."

Another man was with him. Both were hatless, and the sergeant carried a briefcase. If it hadn't been so early she might have taken them for Adventists, or Mormon doorstep preachers.

"We're from the police, Mrs. Lander."

Her eyes widened, one hand to her throat. The sergeant showed his identity card.

"May we come in for a moment?"

"What about?" she said.

American; East Coast, at a guess. "It's just a routine enquiry."

Initial reactions were often the most revealing. As they stepped inside he noted how nervous she was, how defensive. Good looker, but as tense as could be. And what she said next was significant.

"Is it to do with my husband?"

"I couldn't say, Mrs. Lander." He opened his briefcase and

took something out. "Would this be his?" A white luggage tag: H. R. LANDER. "Or is it yours?"

Recognition was immediate, and her heartbeat faltered. The gun case. "It's his," she said, and went to take it. But the sergeant wasn't giving it back to her. "His, yes," she said, trying to brazen over her alarm. "What's so special about a luggage tag?"

"Probably nothing, Mrs. Lander. Is your husband at home?"

"Not right now, no."

Something had happened. They wouldn't have come unless—

"Are you familiar with Shelley's Hotel, Mrs. Lander?"

"I know it."

"Have you stayed there recently?"

"When we live this close?" She shook her head, standing with them in the hallway, courtesies forgotten. Something had happened.

"Has your husband, perhaps?"

"No . . . Why should he?" But she frowned, and he didn't miss it.

"We found the tag at Shelley's."

"Oh?"

"This morning. Outside. It was quite dry, so it probably hadn't been there long." He waited for a reaction. He had the palest eyes she'd ever seen. "This is straight routine, Mrs. Lander. No need to alarm yourself. The tag was on the fire escape at the hotel, and we're merely trying to account for its being there."

Her mind was spinning. The sergeant waited again, without result.

"D'you suppose your husband could have used the hotel at all—for a meal, say?"

On a rising tide of panic she said: "What's this all about? What's so important about a torn-off luggage tag?"

"Could he?"

"It's possible, of course."

"Where does he work, Mrs. Lander?"

"He is on the Defense Attaché's staff at the American Embassy."

"Which is what—a hundred and fifty yards from Shelley's?"

"I suppose so."

The sergeant nodded. "You've been very helpful. We're most grateful." He turned toward the door as if he were on the point of leaving. "Where is your husband now, Mrs. Lander?"

"I . . . I'm not sure."

The hesitation interested him. "Is he traveling?"

"No . . . I don't know."

"Is he absent because of his work?"

"No."

"Why, then? . . . I don't wish to pursue this unnecessarily, but it would be useful in the circumstances if you could tell me why he's not here."

Renata Lander clenched her hands but did not answer.

"When did he go away?"

"Last night." She could hear Noel moving about upstairs. "Late last night."

"For any particular reason?"

Her voice was frozen. "How can this matter to you?"

The other man looked down at his shoes, but the sergeant took it in his stride.

"He packed and left, is that it?"

"No."

"No?"

"We had a row. First he went out and then he came back in and took some money and his jacket and . . . and . . ." She had reached the limit of coherence. "None of this is your concern." She made a distraught gesture. Now it was coming.

"What has any of this to do with Shelley's Hotel and a tag with my husband's name on it?"

"There's been a shooting at the hotel, Mrs. Lander." A sound like surf was roaring in her ears. "Someone's inside with a gun, and all we're doing is following every lead we have in order to find out who he is."

It was the other man who caught her.

7:21 A.M.

THEY HAD taken the drip out of Yorke's left arm and were transfusing him instead.

"Right through," the registrar said, studying the X-ray plates. "Clean as a whistle. He was lucky."

"He could have been luckier still," the nursing sister commented with a brogue straight out of Kerry, "and had the bullet miss him altogether."

"Sometimes, sister, I honestly believe you want us all put out of business."

"Only sometimes?" She pulled the screens round Yorke's bed and smiled grimly. "Would it be such a terrible thing?"

"Heaven on earth?"

"I'd settle for that."

7:26 A.M.

FOUR MINUTES after taking the sergeant's radio call, McConnell's car was screeching to a halt on the cobbles of Bruton Mews. Number 14, a yellow door. The sergeant came outside to meet him, clean-cut, quietly eager, and McConnell saw a glimpse of his own youth there.

"Let's have it again."

"The husband walked out of here last night with a gun. After a row. The tag found on the fire escape came from his gun case—she thinks."

"Only thinks?"

"She flaked out, sir. She's still a bit rocky."

"Take me in, will you?"

Pink-and-grey paper flanking the stairs, some well-framed flower prints on the walls. McConnell's first impression of the sitting room was of neat chintz-covered chairs, velvet curtains, windows that overlooked the mews.

"Mrs. Lander? . . . My name's McConnell."

He left his rank out of it; it was a mouthful, anyway, and she seemed scared enough as it was.

"D'you feel up to talking, Mrs. Lander?"

She nodded, biting her lip. She was extremely pale, sitting upright on the very edge of the couch. A boy was also in the room—thirteen, fourteen—rather bewildered, and McConnell pitied them both. Incredibly, once upon a time, he had managed without feelings.

"Noel," Renata Lander said thickly, "go and get yourself some breakfast, will you?"

The boy went away, not quite closing the door, reluctant to be alone. McConnell said: "D'you mind if I sit down?" The sergeant was there with him. "How long have you lived here, Mrs. Lander?"

"Two years." For some reason she said: "It's rented."

"Your husband's at the Embassy, I understand?" She nodded. "Defense Attaché's department?" She nodded. "And last night he left the house?"

"Yes."

"After an argument?"

"Yes . . . Oh God," she said then. "It can't be what you think. It isn't possible." She buried her face in her hands and seemed to drink from their cup of darkness. "Not Harry . . . Not Harry."

"He took a gun with him, I believe?"

"Yes."

"What kind of gun?"

"A rifle."

"What kind of rifle?"

She shook her head. "He belongs to a club at Lancaster Gate."

"Was the rifle always kept here?"

"Except for Thursday evenings. Club evenings."

McConnell twisted the wedding ring on his finger. "How bad was the argument you had last night?"

"Awful. But Harry would never do what you're thinking. It doesn't make sense. We were cat and dog last night, sure, and I'll never forgive myself, but Harry isn't capable—"

"Have you rowed at other times?"

"Yes."

"Often?"

"Quite often."

"And he's walked out on you? . . . He's done what he did last night?"

"Yes."

"Stayed out?"

"Not before this."

"How long've you been married, Mrs. Lander?"

"Fifteen years."

"Has he struck you ever?"

"No." Her eyes flashed.

"Threatened you?"

"No."

"Would you say your husband is a violent man?"

"No." Then again: "No."

"What was the argument about?"

She shifted uneasily, in the grip of dread and disbelief. "Many things." There were tears on her cheeks. "Many, many things."

Too early to start probing into that; first things first. "What sort of build is your husband, Mrs. Lander?"

"Tall, broad . . . A hundred and eighty, around that. Dark-haired."

"And what was he wearing?"

"I told the sergeant—he came back for his jacket."

"At what time?"

"Half past twelve?"

"How long after he first went out?"

"I couldn't say for sure." Her fingers were at war with each other. "I was—well, I'd gone to sleep. He came back in for his jacket and some money and the gun case."

"What sort of jacket is it? What color?"

"It's a black-and-white check," she said.

7:38 A.M.

THE GUN WAS a focal point. That, and his eyes—the changing wildness in them, the cunning, the fleeting moments of sheer emptiness. On and off he paced the room like an animal. To Gabrielle Wilding it had begun to seem that there had never been a time when they weren't at the mercy of his will, never an instant when fear was only a split second short of terror. It would be lunacy to disobey; suicide.

She lay down. He didn't object. He had moved closer to the door, and by turning to her left she managed to put him out of her sight; Ireland as well. She had a contempt for Ireland now that would last as long as she lived. The various paths that had finally brought her to his bed were peopled by men who were never put to any test except that of their mutual satisfaction, yet she couldn't think of one who would have been so spineless. Not one, not even that idiot in the architect's office who failed in other ways . . .

The irony had no end. Ireland played Nick Sudden, coolly immaculate in a Chester Barrie suit, supreme in a riverside penthouse, private eye par excellence, sexually insatiable and physically indestructible. Five television series in as many years had merged Richard Ireland and Nick Sudden in the public mind, and she had gone along with the deception like everybody else. Willingly; blindly. Swallowed it whole, gone further than all but a few and, within a limited arena, found no difference between the role he played and the abilities he possessed.

Until now. Make-believe was useless now.

She should have escaped while the chance was there. And it *was* there, nothing to stop her. . . . On the bed she tried to pray, a kind of prayer, the language of it never learned. A pigeon began to purr-purr on a nearby sill, the softest sound of summer, and for half a moment she almost didn't believe in the police positioned in the corridor outside or the hovering threat of the situation in the room.

Only for half a moment, though.

"One day," her mother used to say, "you'll land yourself in a heap of trouble, girl. Mark my words. There was a time when you called this house a home, but it's not to your liking any more." A railwayman's cottage near Reading. "We're not smart enough for you nowadays. . . ."

"Phil?"

"Yeah?"

"Heard the news?"

"They've done away with VAT—that it?"

" 'Bout Ireland. Richard Ireland."

"What about him?"

"He's one of the hostages at Shelley's. . . . It's true, Phil. He's caught up in the Shelley's thing."

"You using a code or something? Whatever it is, you're

82

going too fast for me. Can't you try again nearer dictation speed? I'm just his agent, remember, and no use to man or beast before ten."

He listened without visible astonishment, blue-jowled and balding, perched naked on the fat rim of the bath.

"He's collecting himself fantastic publicity, Phil. Sensational."

"I'm with you."

"The new series due and all."

"I'm with you. But isn't he in the hell of a spot? If there's been shooting—right?—and if some crazy—"

"The police are playing it cat and mouse, Phil. Just a couple of minutes ago they were as good as assuring me—"

"Who's the girl?"

"Someone by the name of Wilding."

"Doesn't he ever try the pleasures of an empty room, that man?"

"He's a bag of cats, all right."

"And married," Phil said. "And off the top of my head right now I'd say he needs a girl in this the way Custer needed a few more Indians."

7:52 A.M.
"WE'VE GOT to go on, Mrs. Lander," McConnell insisted. "Now. Lives are at stake."

"It can't be Harry." She pressed the knuckles of her fists together, red-eyed, shaking her head. "*Can't* be, no matter what. Harry's not a killer." The word alone seemed to shock her. "When he left here—"

"When he left here he took a gun with him—not immediately, but as soon as makes no difference. He also took a jacket with a distinctive check. The tag with his name on it came from the gun case and was found on Shelley's fire escape.

During the night a man was seen in Shelley's wearing a jacket like your husband's, and there's someone in there now with a gun—and two hostages. . . . These are facts, known facts."

"Even so it can't be him. . . . *No*." She would be loyal to the last, he knew; so often they were. "It's impossible."

"What did you row about?" He lifted his shoulders slightly. "Money?"

"Everything."

"A woman?"

"In part."

"Is there another woman?"

"There was." Her look said these were secrets. "Not any more."

"Are you certain?"

"Yes."

"Had he been drinking?"

"Yes."

"Heavily?"

"No more than usual."

"Does he have a drink problem?"

"The last year or so." She nodded. He'd changed so much, always under strain. "You could say that."

"What state was he in when he left the house? In any way abnormal?"

"He just stormed out," she said. She could see him still, hear him still, hear herself. "That wouldn't make him do what you say."

"He came back for his gun, Mrs. Lander." How loose her mouth was. "Is there any history of mental disturbance in his record?"

"*No!*" Her voice lifted.

"Not that you know of? No psychological disorder?"

"No."

"Anything you might have said that could have triggered what's happened?" She didn't reply, fighting tears, and he made the point again. "A lot of what we know adds up, Mrs. Lander."

"You're wrong," she maintained in desperation. "You have to be wrong."

McConnell knew something about the indestructibility of hope. "Will you help me?"

"How?"

"Speak to him."

"It isn't him."

"Speak to whoever's there." He noticed the boy in the crack of the door, eavesdropping. "Have your son speak to him."

"I don't see—"

"Listen, Mrs. Lander. There are a man and woman in a fifth-floor room at Shelley's, held at gunpoint. Why, I don't know. What the gunman has in mind I don't know. I've tried to make contact, but without success. And I need to reach him; it's imperative. If not personally, then through someone else."

"Noel has to go to school." Only somebody clinging to normality could have said it. "To the Lycée."

"Is Harry a good father?"

Her lips trembled. "He's a marvelous father."

"I want someone to help me coax him out of there," McConnell said.

It was terrible to watch the doubt beginning visibly to show itself in the depths of her eyes, but he started working on what he saw.

"I have a dual responsibility, Mrs. Lander. To the hostages and to the man who's got a gun on them. If only I can appeal to that man—calm him in some way, satisfy him, persuade him to abandon what he's doing—then I've achieved my objective.

Whoever that man is, whatever the reasons for his being there."

He paused a few seconds, using the silence like a weapon.

"The alternative can only mean more shooting. Perhaps three deaths." He was talking to a woman whose world was in ribbons and whose bruised-looking gaze was almost impossible to hold. "I think it's your husband, Mrs. Lander. All the evidence points that way, though God grant I'm wrong." He threw that in. "Somehow I've got to turn the key that's made him do this thing, help him to unlock himself, reach him somehow. . . . And I can't do it on my own."

8:00 A.M.

DANNAHAY arrived at the Embassy an hour before his usual time. He came in from the Kensington direction—Hyde Park Corner, Park Lane, Deanery Street and South Audley Street. No problems, no sign of anything unusual until he swung the Mustang toward the underground garage chute in Blackburne's Mews and saw the blue caravan and the police cars.

He took the stairs up to the main entrance lobby and produced his pass for the Marine guard at the desk.

"What've I been missing? Why all the fuzz suddenly?"

"There's been shooting around here. One old guy shot dead over near the Navy Building and a policeman wounded in Shelley's Hotel."

"You don't say?"

"Whoever's got the itchy finger is up in a room there with a couple of hostages right now, playing hard to get."

"That so?"

"Radio's been full of it," the Marine said pointedly.

"It's a wicked world." Dannahay tossed and caught his car keys. "I prefer listening to music."

He rode in the elevator up to the second. JOHN B. DANNAHAY,

86

it said on the door of his office, LEGAL ATTACHE. It was a fair-sized office, obsessionally tidy, a photograph of the President on one of the walls, a map of the world on another. The windows gave him a view of the Roosevelt Memorial through the leafy plane and lime trees in the square: he went straight over to them and peered left, instantly aware of the total absence of traffic, no one to be seen except a couple of men by the Navy Building. He pulled the fawn-colored curtains a little aside and opened the window, struck by the abnormal quiet.

The men positioned at the corner were armed; no bones about that. London was changing. Rather you than me, he thought, and turned away, no involvement, something else on his mind.

He kept his office keys on a thin silver chain. From the metal cabinet in the corner of the room he took a couple of bulky files and laid them on his desk. If only Knollenberg had managed something better with the camera they could terminate today: they were that close. If necessary they could still take action on the basis of the proof they already had—and he was under some pressure to make his move. But—Christ—it was going to stink when the time came, and he'd rather dot every eye and cross every tee before that happened.

"So," he said to himself, pulled in the swivel chair and started working through the first of the files from the beginning.

8:09 A.M.
"Is IT CORRECT that you believe the gunman's an American?"

"No comment," Llewellyn said.

He was in the doorway of the caravan, a dozen newspapermen crowding close, and he was stalling.

"Is it correct that you are now aware of the gunman's identity?"

"No comment."

"What *do* you know about the gunman?" This was Kent. "And if he *is* an American citizen, what special liaison do you have with the American authorities?"

"At the moment, gentlemen, I am not in a position to answer these questions. I'm sorry, but that's the way it is. We *are* working on certain deductions and taking a particular course of action, and a full statement will be issued at the very earliest opportunity. That's all I'm prepared to say at this point."

The man from the *Mirror* never gave up. "Can you confirm that Chief Superintendent McConnell is currently questioning a woman in connection with the Shelley's situation?"

"I'm sorry," Llewellyn said. He smiled thinly and went inside, beyond range.

Noel and Renata Lander were in the back of McConnell's car, with McConnell in the front seat alongside the driver, screwed round so as to talk with them.

"When we arrive, Mrs. Lander, I'll go with you both up to the fifth floor and I'll stay with you while you use the hailer. You'll be quite safe. There are men posted—"

"Isn't he my husband?" It was pitiful.

"I'm sorry."

They passed the Connaught on their right, Mount Street all shapes of sunlight and shadow, the three of them blind to it.

"What do I say?"

"Anything, anything at all that you feel will persuade him to come out . . . He's probably frightened, Mrs. Lander. Reassurance is possibly what he needs most. Remind him of who he is. . . ."

She was crying again, no tears, but with her shoulders shaking. And the boy looked stunned, a tight grip on his mother's arm. God knows what awful state their minds were in, and whether, in the deepest recesses of themselves, they were somehow clinging to the hems of hope.

No longer, surely, McConnell thought. Not any more.

They turned through the motorcycle checkpoints at the junction of Park Street and Lees Place. Some early commuters had gathered already and they stared into the car, wooden and unaware. The driver zigzagged at speed into the service area at the back of Shelley's, and as they all got out a flash bulb popped, making them blink.

"This way."

McConnell led them into the foyer via the kitchens and the dining room. There was some activity in the kitchen, and a number of people were at tables in the dining room. To Renata Lander it was unreal to find them there, unreal to pass through into the foyer and its buzz of activity, unreal to take the elevator and emerge into the silence that greeted them on the fifth floor, unreal to have accepted the connection between this corridor and Bruton Mews—terribly, starkly unreal.

Savage motioned them to join him where the stairs led down, and McConnell picked up the bullhorn.

"Hold it like this"—he showed Renata Lander—"and press the button when you speak."

She nodded, a shrinking sensation deep in her stomach as she looked at the one closed door along the corridor and saw the partly hidden men to either side of it.

Then she lifted the bullhorn and held it with both hands. "Harry?" she began, a shuddered breath between. "Harry? . . ."

He stopped pacing the room the moment she spoke. His eyes narrowed. The girl sat up, and Ireland cocked his head.

89

Strain was on all their faces, different questions and apprehensions.

"Please listen to me, Harry...."

He snorted, and his mouth curled. But he listened, standing with his legs apart, the rifle held across his hips.

"Noel is with me, right here with me now. And both of us are asking you the same thing—we want you to come out, Harry.... We want you back with us."

It wasn't possible to decipher what was in his expression. Guilt, was it? Scorn?

"Please, Harry ... Listen, Harry ..."

Anger?

Renata Lander began to speak about things that had been with her since marriage, about love and pain and misunderstanding, about things shared and things denied, hesitant to begin with, faltering, sometimes lost for words, sometimes borne on a torrent of them. There was a terrible passion and poignancy in all she said, and her voice vibrated down the corridor and into the room where no one moved.

"Do you remember that time in Paris, Harry? That vacation? Noel was small and we left him with my mother—d'you remember? And what happened when we got to the hotel and found we had that awful Scotsman's luggage? ..."

He grunted then. "Fool," they thought he muttered, white showing in his eyes. But he went on listening, didn't contort his face like the last time and shout that he wanted it ended; no sign of the frightening eruption of rage which had loosed off a shot into the bathroom. He seemed fascinated, yet untouched, almost as if the appeals were meant for somebody else.

"Come on out, Harry. Come out and be with Noel and me."

She spoke with more and more emotion, approaching breakdown, jerking from one pause to another, talking of the past and of the future—although the future now could only be some other kind of nightmare.

"If you love us, Harry . . . *Please,* Harry . . ."

In the room they looked at him and saw she was making no impression. And Gabrielle Wilding covered her ears, distressed more than she could bear by another's anguish.

McConnell touched Renata Lander gently on the arm and took the bullhorn from her, hating that part of him which had used her—and which would use her again if it seemed worthwhile. No one should have heard what they had listened to except the man it was intended for; or witnessed what it had cost her.

She sobbed quietly. "It's no good. . . . No good."

"Let your son try." McConnell turned to the boy, no other weapons at his command. "Will you, Noel?"

"Yes, sir."

"Just a few words. Just to confirm that you're here."

"It's me, Dad—Noel . . ."

In the room he frowned, eyes flicking to and fro.

". . . and we want you to come and join us out here."

For a few seconds something seemed to go wrong with the bullhorn. There was a series of amplified clicks before the boy spoke again.

"How about this one, Dad?" It was Michael Caine to begin with. "The Owl and the Pussy-Cat went to sea in a beautiful pea-green boat. They took some honey, and plenty of money . . ."

The frown lessened slightly.

". . . wrapped up in a five-pound note."

Outside, in the corridor, they watched the door beyond the scattered corn flakes. In the room they stayed stock still. Richard Ireland's mouth was gaping. Noel Lander switched to Cagney, bravely and with heartbreak, tears in the voice.

"Listen to me, you dirty rat . . ."

There was more reaction now. Gabrielle Wilding watched as a spasm shook him. Suddenly he was disturbed, agitated again.

"Get it stopped"—like a razor slash.

She snatched up the phone and spoke to Helen Olivares, who passed the message to the man posted in the room across the corridor from the place where Noel was speaking.

"That's enough, son," McConnell said urgently. "That'll do."

"Yes?" Helen Olivares asked a second later. "What's the other thing?"

"He wants to speak with the American Ambassador," she was told nervously. "The American Ambassador, right."

8:23 A.M.
"CAN I SEE HIM?" Dysart asked the plump blonde nurse.

"He isn't conscious yet. There's no point, really."

"He'll be okay, though?"

"I'm sure he will," she said, new and junior and not too good at this. "Are you a relative?"

Dysart shook his head. "Colleague."

"Were you with him at the time?"

"No."

Directly Dysart was released from duty he had rung home to say that he'd be late, and then come here.

He found himself saying: "He was going to be best man at a wedding this afternoon."

"Was he?"

"He won't be doing that, of course."

She smiled: the big men were the worst. "Hardly."

"But he'll be okay?" She could tell him a hundred times

92

and he'd still not quite believe it; anxiety did that to you. "He'll pull out of this all right, won't he?"

"Sure," the nurse said. "Why not come back later and see for yourself?"

8:28 A.M.

McCONNELL was through to Commander Trethowan, speaking from 509, the disheveled bed in there only part of the evidence of hasty evacuation two hours and more ago.

"Any reason given?" Trethowan asked, no-stone-unturned-Trethowan.

"He doesn't give reasons, sir. And we don't speak to him direct. He makes the girl do the talking."

"I'll contact Osborne at the Embassy. This is beginning to tread on their toes."

"But warn them, will you? There's only one answer the Ambassador can reasonably give. And he's got to be quick about giving it."

"Who exactly is Lander?"

"He's on the Defense Attaché's staff."

"Would the Ambassador know him, d'you reckon?"

McConnell bit off the retort that sprang to his lips. "With the lives of two hostages in the balance, that hardly matters. Lander wants words with him, and that does."

Mulholland was at breakfast, black coffee and assorted vitamin pills, when Osborne called him. Andrew Osborne was the Marine guard commander: hidebound, inflexible.

"Lander?" Yes, he knew Lander, Mulholland said, and listened. "Good Christ," he exclaimed presently, "you can't be serious." He listened again, eyebrows arched like caterpillars. "What made 'em decide it's him? . . . Uh-huh . . . Uh-huh . . . Well, this is terrible. Terrible."

"He's asking to speak with you, Mr. Ambassador."

"If that's what he wants, of course. But—"

"I'd say it's more of a demand."

"What's he have in mind, d'you know?"

"No, sir."

"No idea?"

"None at all."

"He's got a wife, hasn't he? Wife and teen-age son, as far as I recall."

"That's correct, yes."

"Are they aware of the situation?"

"I understand so."

"God help them." Mulholland sucked in air. "You've flung it at me so fast that I find it almost impossible to believe—you know that? . . . What in the world's gotten into him?"

"I'm in no position to express a view on that, sir." Andrew Osborne's god was action. "May I suggest you agree to speak with him right away?"

"Of course, of course. I'll do that." He shot a glance at his watch. "But I'd rather have it happen from the Embassy."

"How soon from now?"

"Nine o'clock?"

"Can I tell the police not later than nine o'clock? They're the ones at the sharp end of the problem."

"Right."

"You *will* speak to Lander and not later than nine o'clock?" Osborne wanted no misunderstanding. "Is that correct, sir?"

"Correct, yes . . . And listen," Mulholland added. "Have Sam O'Hare be there with me. Sam O'Hare and Robbie Ryder. I want them in on this."

"Very well." Minister and Defense Attaché, respectively. "I'll see they're alerted."

"And I want a tape run on Lander and me."

"He's speaking through one of the hostages."

"Even so."

"Right, sir."

"One last thing," Mulholland said. "George, is it? George Lander? . . . I forget."

"Harry," Osborne told him.

8:38 A.M.

DANNAHAY was a third of the way through the first of the files. He had slipped his jacket off and loosened his tie, and his feet were resting on the end of the big desk.

"Morning," Knollenberg said, there without a knock.

"You're early."

"Better'n the other way round, I guess."

"We said nine."

"I'm an enthusiast," Knollenberg said. "Don't tell me you hadn't noticed." He crossed the room and put his briefcase alongside Dannahay's feet. "Anyway, what about you?"

"I'm unmarried," Dannahay said.

"But not unloved."

"Who's as sharp as a knife this morning, eh?"

Knollenberg took a yellow folder from the briefcase and spread the matte prints on the desk. They were identical, the man framed in the doorway of the Vagabond Club.

Dannahay puckered his nose. "And that's it?"

"That's it."

He turned toward the window. "We'll have to go inside the place. If they won't come out together, then someone's got to go on in and be there with them at the tables."

"Agreed, John. Been thinking the same thing."

"Any problems?"

"Wouldn't say so. I'll have to inquire, of course. Off the

cuff I'd say a miniature could do it well enough, but I'll have to see what's what." He used his hands. "In the button-hole, maybe—yes?"

"Something like that."

"I'll find out. When d'you figure—forty-eight hours?"

"Next time he goes there," Dannahay said. "It's getting time we shut up the shop, once and for all."

"Okay."

Someone rapped on the door and came in—Jake Shaw-cross, the Press Officer. "You guys heard?"

"A clue would help. Our mind-reading days are over."

"This fellow gone crazy with a gun over there at Shel-ley's . . ." Four times already, in twice as many minutes, he'd relished these moments of drama. "It's Lander, Harry Lander. *Yeah* . . . How about that for starters?"

Knollenberg was absolutely bewildered. "What fellow gone crazy with a gun? . . . Say, what *is* this? What's going on around here?"

8:52 A.M.

HOME? Go home? Oh no, oh God no . . . Renata Lander shook her head. She swallowed the brandy they had brought her. Home was out of the question. *Wait* there, did McConnell mean?

"I want to stay in the hotel," she said.

"It's just as you wish."

"I've got to be here."

They had gone into a room at the other end of the corridor on the fifth. She was beyond tears now, and her eyes seemed enormous in the drawn structure of her face. Wherever she turned, whichever way she looked, Harry's parting expression was there to haunt her.

"What can he want with the Ambassador?"

In a daze she sat down, baffled and wounded by the rejection of her appeals. Silence was a terrible answer, and it was never his way to be silent. Or to kill, she thought, the enormity of the shock as savage as ever. She covered her face again, still trying to grapple with the reasons why their lives had somehow converged on this meaningless place, on two rooms, this one with its lingering smell of strangers.

"If you'll excuse me, Mrs. Lander," McConnell said, leaving. "I'll have someone come up to be with you."

"That . . . won't be necessary."

"I'd rather you weren't alone. And, of course, it's possible we shall need you again."

The quiet was intense when he'd gone and the door was shut. Just the two of them there, Noel and herself, and everything seemed unreal again, unbelievable. Noel came and put an arm around her shoulders, Noel, who would normally have left the house for school but instead had tried to entice his father into making a response with those corny impressions. It tore at her heart to think of it.

Bravely, but with absolutely no conviction, Noel said: "Everything'll be all right. . . . Just you wait and see."

He bit on his lower lip, frightened, needing the contact with her. And she needed him as well, more than at any time she'd ever known.

"I love him, Noel. I love your father."

"So do I."

"And I love you too." She could hear the thudding of her pulse as she held him close. "Remember that, whatever happens."

8:55 A.M.

WHEN THE Ambassador was first mentioned, Ireland and the girl had thought he wasn't serious.

Every minute of the past three hours had been part of an endless postponement of his aims and intentions, and the suddenness of his demand to Helen Olivares took them by surprise. They knew so much about how he looked and how he moved and how he spoke, but where his mind was sometimes and what, in the unpredictability of his madness, he was after remained a mystery.

"Remind 'em," he jerked at Gabrielle Wilding. "Tell 'em Mulholland's got exactly five minutes more."

His accent straddled the Atlantic. He kicked his heels impatiently against the wall, standing there between two of the Nolan prints, watching all the time. The day was burning bright outside, but everything here was sepia dark and cigarette smoke stung the eyes.

"You know the Ambassador?" he asked them.

"No."

He didn't want an answer; he asked for asking's sake, part of the tension, nerves at work on him as surely as on them.

At the other end of the line Helen Olivares was saying: "Any moment now I'm expecting to connect you."

"Make it soon," the girl urged, not passing on the message.

"I've a line open to the American Embassy, and they're very clear about the situation."

With the receiver held away from her head he could hear all this. "Two minutes," he said now, a muscle flicking in his cheek. "Two minutes and that's all. Tell 'em and tell 'em quick. I've had my fill of waiting."

Ireland's nausea rose in his stomach again. He lurched abruptly from the bed toward the bathroom, hands aloft as if in frantic surrender. Simultaneously the rifle came up, the face above it reflexed with alarm, never more dangerous than when startled.

"Yes?" Gabrielle Wilding said.

"The Ambassador's on the line." A moment's delay ensued. Then he was there, gruff and cautious. "Hullo, hullo—this is Ralph Mulholland."

She gestured desperately across the room.

"Harry?" Mulholland ventured, O'Hare and Ryder close by, the tape picking it up. "What's all the trouble, Harry?"

"Tell him I've got an important matter to discuss."

Gabrielle Wilding passed the message, verbatim.

"Sure," Mulholland said. "I'm only too anxious to help. Go right ahead."

"Tell him it's a personal matter."

"Fine . . . So why not leave the lady out of it? Why not talk with me direct? To be honest, I'd prefer it that way. For one thing, it's less cumbersome, Harry."

All this back and forth between the three of them. In the bathroom the sound of retching ended and the cistern flushed.

"Tell him that's the way I want it too."

"Fine." The silences were bristling, electric. "That's a good beginning, Harry. Let's keep it going in the same vein."

"In here."

Gabrielle Wilding frowned, repeating what he'd said.

"In here." He jabbed a finger at the floor and delivered his bombshell. "I want Mulholland in this room. In person. And I give him an hour to make it. . . . Now tell him that."

9:04 A.M.

ROBERTO OLIVARES sat stiffly in the padded chair with his mouth wide open and Gilbert's arms about his neck. He was lucky, Gilbert had told him in direct Australian fashion, to be there without an appointment; very, very lucky.

"It's an altogether third-rate tooth." The probe and mirror concentrated on only one area. "And it'll have to come out."

"So."

"In return for which I expect ᵗ⁀ be told exactly what's going on at Shelley's. From the inside."

Roberto Olivares grunted.

"Tell you the truth, I'm surprised to see you here at all. In the circumstances—as I know them—I'd have thought the manager would be up to his eyes."

"Helen—"

"What's that?"

With his mouth full of metal Roberto Olivares did his best to explain that he had an extraordinarily capable wife.

"You won't comply, surely?"

This was O'Hare, tall and bronzed and the smartest dresser of the three, grey hair complementing his dark-blue suit.

"Seems I've got no choice, Sam."

Ryder, the Defense Attaché, didn't speak, but he shook his head.

"What's the alternative?" Mulholland said gravely.

"Someone's got to damp him down . . . distract him."

"That's easier said than done."

"If you go into that room you not only level a gun at your own head, you automatically tie the hands of everyone on the outside. We'll be ripe for every demand under the sun."

"Aren't we now?"

"Not to the same extent."

"No?"

"Not in my book," O'Hare said doggedly.

Mulholland raised his eyes to Ryder. "What does your book say, Robbie? You know Lander better than the rest of us."

They were in his office at the Embassy, the inner office with the Navajo blanket paintings that he admired so much, and the sense of urgency was on them all.

"Up until yesterday I'd have gone along with that. But

now . . ." Ryder hunched his shoulders. "It's possible he can be reasoned with."

"Look, he's *killed* a man," O'Hare argued, "and he's put a bullet—"

"I'm up to date on what he's done."

"The police have tried the reasoning bit and failed. His wife and son have tried as well."

"Sure, but he never sought to contact *them*. With the Ambassador it's different. This time Lander's made the approach himself, and I say it's possible, just possible—"

"'Approach'—Jesus! You're using the wrong kind of language."

Their voices were sharpening an edge, and Mulholland intervened. "Who cares about the language? I understand Robbie's point even if you don't."

"I understand his point too, but I don't for one minute think you should go into that room. It'd be madness."

Mulholland gestured heavily. "Let's cool it, shall we, and just concern ourselves with the facts? I say again—what's the alternative?"

"That's for the British to answer. Back home—"

"Are we always so clever back home?"

Ryder said: "I'd go in myself if Lander would accept me. He's my man, after all. He's my responsibility. Whatever's gotten into him is something—"

"Thanks, Robbie. But it isn't you he wants. And his deadline's around ten—one hour from when he made the girl hang up."

"I'm calling Whitehall," O'Hare said abruptly. "The police need to be pressured into taking more positive action. With only an hour to play with, their kind of waiting game's out." Impulsively, he turned to the window and angled the Venetian blinds against the sun's almost horizontal rays. "An hour's no time at all."

Mulholland was looking at the photograph of his family on the desk. "That depends," he said, "how close you are to the gun."

The smell of sweat was in the room now, Ireland's and hers and his, the stale air sharp with the tang of it.

"He'd better come." His fingers were restless on the trigger guard and his eyes glinted in the lamplight. "God help you if Mulholland doesn't show."

He took a box of shells from a bulging pocket in his jacket, and Gabrielle Wilding looked away, unable to watch the turmoil in him and still keep any sort of hold on herself.

9:09 A.M.

"Yes, sir," McConnell said to the Commissioner of Police. "Exactly, sir." He listened some more before saying: "It's been attempted, sir. We've done our best in that direction."

"Try again."

"Of course. But I can't lean on him. He's too unstable for that. I can keep him reminded that he's surrounded, and I've every hope that time will wear him down. Beyond that, at the moment—"

"This demand for the American Ambassador to become a third hostage has somehow got to be side-stepped."

"I don't see how, sir. If Lander persists with the demand, then it seems to me we have very little choice and will have to put it to the Ambassador, fair and square. He's being kept in constant—"

"And if the Ambassador refuses?"

"I'll come to that bridge at ten o'clock, sir."

"The Home Secretary is pressing me to give him an assurance—"

McConnell cut in. "I'd rather have three live people in there

102

with Lander than a couple of dead ones. A dozen, even. And I don't mind who they are. Time's the one thing on my side. It's a flimsy-enough weapon, God knows, but I've got to use it. And if the Ambassador can buy us a little more, well and good. Once he's in there he'll be my prime consideration, the way the others are now."

For a long moment there was silence. Then, as though he'd come to a decision with himself, the Commissioner said: "Thank you, McConnell."

"Sir?"

"Keep trying. Keep what pressure on you can."

"Very good, sir."

McConnell hung up. He was in the far corner of the caravan with Llewellyn, and the low ceiling made him stoop a little. Llewellyn creased his face and said: "Some are more equal than others?"

"Not really," McConnell answered. He started to leave. "No, I wouldn't say that."

Outside, Kent was the first to try his luck. "Anything you can give me, Chief Superintendent?"

"Nothing you don't already know."

"Is it correct that Lander's demanding Ralph Mulholland as a third hostage?"

"I reckon that one's for the Press Officer at the Embassy, don't you?"

He broke into a run across Upper Brook Street, heading for Shelley's.

9:14 A.M.
"MARY KAY?"

Mulholland was alone. O'Hare and Ryder had left at his request. "Five, ten minutes—that's all . . . I want to speak with my wife." After they'd withdrawn he had stood for a while in deep thought, somehow incredulous, a big man with a fine square face that was printed with a map of many inner journeys, none more demanding than now.

Then he'd pressed the switch and asked for Winfield House. "Ralph?"

He guessed she was still at breakfast, in her room.

"I need your help, Mary Kay." No time to waste, but every syllable from the heart. "You've got to tell me what to do."

"Listen, Lander . . . what d'you hope to gain by having your ambassador come in there? How's it going to benefit you?"

McConnell's voice brayed from the bullhorn, vibrant in the narrow corridor.

"What will it change as far as you're concerned? There'll still be a score of marksmen waiting for you—out here, across the street, in the rooms on either side of you. Below you, above you. You're surrounded, Lander. So what's the point?"

He was as near to a threat as he dared to bring himself. Yet a threat at this stage was empty, and he knew it—just as the Commissioner knew it once he was out of range of the politicians. For the time being the man in 501 held the whip hand.

"You've got two people in there, but you've no more hope of changing things with three than with two. . . . Why not come out now and join your wife and son?"

A shot punctured the door, wood splintering. Everyone in the corridor went rigid, motionless, pressed into openings. They'd had this answer before. For seconds on end there was no sound except for the hum of the air-conditioning, silence along the entire floor until Renata Lander came bursting out of the room she was in at the end of the corridor.

"Harry? . . . Harry?"

And at ground level, far below, Helen Olivares was taking a shrill phone message.

"He wants that policeman's tongue torn out. . . . That's what he says," Gabrielle Wilding breathed hysterically, the natural rhythm all distorted. "It's our last chance, he says. He wants no more of it. . . . No more, from the police or anyone else."

"I'm telling them, girl, I'm telling them."

"There . . . there's something else. . . . Mulholland's used up more than a quarter of his time already."

9:19 A.M.
"RALPH, RALPH . . . You're the one who must decide."

"I can't. Not by myself. I haven't the right."

"Nor have I."

"There are no two ways about this, Mary Kay. Unless they can get Lander to change his mind, I must either go in or refuse to go in. It's that simple."

He spelled it out for her again, balancing the threat against the consequences, nothing dramatized, just the facts, the plain, frightening facts.

And eventually, reluctantly, still grappling with the suddenness of everything, she said: "You've no choice, Ralph."

"As a private person?"

She caught her breath a little. "As a dear, beloved private person . . . you've still no choice."

"Thanks, Mary Kay."

"I'm coming over."

"I may not be here."

"All the same I'm coming. Just as soon as I can manage. I'll be close. All the time I'll be close. Remember that."

"Sure," he said.

Words alone had a terrible inadequacy. He needed her presence, the feel of her, the look of her: for thirty years it had been so. She was the rock on which he'd built his life.

105

"I'm going to pray that it doesn't happen . . . that it doesn't need to happen. Are you there, Ralph?"

"Yes."

"God bless and protect you. And I'll be close—don't forget."

"Thanks, Mary Kay."

He rang off, an element of disbelief still with him, even now. Then the buzzer sounded on the desk and he pressed the switch.

"Yes?"

"The Foreign Secretary's on the line, Mr. Ambassador."

9:24 A.M.

YORKE opened his eyes and gazed without focusing at the blurred shapes confronting him. He made an effort to focus, but could not; made an effort to move, but could not. Where he was he didn't understand, though a sullen pain in his right shoulder dragged his thoughts toward the hazy recollection of a violent, scalding blow and the sense of falling into darkness.

And more besides.

"Man," he said, mouth so dry that no sound came.

The blurred blue-and-white shape his body's length away moved closer, and he made out a face, a girl's face. He licked his lips, eyes staring, the trained part of his mind struggling desperately to surface.

"Man," he said thickly. "Man in a check jacket. Two other people in the room."

"Hallo." The nurse smiled.

"Another man and a—"

"Easy now, easy. That's all taken care of. So relax . . ."

MULHOLLAND wrote the message on a sheet of paper and handed it to his secretary. *All will be well, and keeping your fingers crossed will help to make it so. Press reports certain to exaggerate. Your mother and I will be thinking of you. A father's love. Ralph.*

"Cable that to my son and daughter when ten o'clock comes."

"Yes, sir."

"And keep your own fingers crossed as well."

"All of us here will be doing that."

He had never seen his secretary show emotion before. He had no strong sense of doom, of last things. Not like Anzio, all those years ago. He even managed a grim smile. He knew Lander. A stranger would be different; terrifying. But Lander? Lander and he at least shared common ground. Yet as O'Hare and Ryder re-entered the office he was conscious of a growing nervousness, a feeling of inevitability. Whenever he looked at his watch time seemed to be accelerating.

O'Hare said strongly: "I still feel you should back off. The British should make you hard to get. I hate this giving in to a man's demands without so much as stalling tactics."

"Two lives are in the balance, Sam. He's made it very clear."

"Bluff."

"With one man shot dead already? The police know what they're doing. Let's face it—"

"Why in God's name has he picked on you?"

"For a start, I suppose, because he's an American." Mulholland shrugged, the inner tension building up. "Which, you could say, is my bad luck."

"More to the point," Ryder said, frowning, "is what's turned Lander homicidal, overnight at that."

Anything could have done it, Mulholland thought. Back in Philadelphia last year a person went on the rampage over the way his wife set the places at the table. He said: "Everyone has a breaking point."

"And a point of no return?"

"I'll come out of there, don't worry."

He leaned across the desk and buzzed his secretary in the outer office. "Get me Washington, please. The White House." A direct line was at his disposal, and he was reaching for the red telephone as he spoke, something begun at midnight in another man's mind now controlling his own.

"The police have asked you to be in the hotel lobby by quarter of." This was O'Hare. The sunburst clock on the wall was showing four minutes after the half-hour.

Mulholland nodded, emptying his pockets of everything except cigarettes and a handkerchief, pen and aspirins. He hesitated over a nail file, then put it aside. "Osborne's still liaising with the police—right?"

"Right."

"Don't you think that's really John Dannahay's pigeon now we're going to be—sort of—off limits?" It was a wry phrase to use, but the suggestion was shrewd. "I've a feeling his experience is better accustomed to this sort of emergency."

"I'll speak with him," O'Hare agreed.

"No reflection on Andrew, but I reckon John will have more to offer. No reflection on the British either, but I reckon John's a good brain for anyone to pick."

"I'll speak with him," O'Hare said again. "He'll jump at it."

"How do I get over to the hotel? Do we walk or ride?"

"Ride."

For an hour he had been in ceaseless demand, one interruption after another. "I have your White House connection," his secretary was saying then.

THEY WENT down to the basement garage and boarded the Cadillac, all three, Mulholland, O'Hare and Ryder. Seconds earlier another black car made a diversionary run, two of Osborne's staff in the rear, drawing the cameramen's fire—flash, flash. All the world was watching now.

The Cadillac swept up the incline into Blackburne's Mews, Mulholland's new driver at the wheel, and swung away from the groups gathered close to the police headquarters caravan. They were seen, but not impeded, turning clockwise into Upper Grosvenor Street and then Park Street, speeding toward Lees Place.

The warmth of the day was already in the streets, in their pores. There were people three deep at the police barriers across the intersections, and at one of them Mulholland glimpsed the gaunt figure of a placard-bearer—PREPARE TO MEET THY GOD—like something meant for him and him alone.

Lees Place was deserted, printed with blocks of shadow, the upper part of Shelley's showing ahead. The driver brought the Cadillac sidling softly into the hotel's service area, the place all bustle now, another pack of photographers in evidence, biding their time.

O'Hare swore, but Mulholland was resigned to them. Some burly policemen moved forward and kept a way clear through the crush into the back of the hotel, a babble of voices all around. Then Osborne appeared with Trethowan—"This way, sir, this way"—everything arranged, guiding Mulholland and the others past the delivery bays and the cold storage into the undermanned kitchen and the nearly empty dining room, hints of routine and normality everywhere despite the stares, despite the whispers.

The Commissioner greeted them in the foyer. He was waiting there with McConnell, uniformed, an element of protocol in the formality of his manner and the presence of a grey-faced individual from the Foreign Office whose name was lost in the terse introductions and expressions of regret. The foyer had been cleared and one of the elevators was waiting, ready to load and go up.

McConnell didn't indulge in any preliminaries. "I'm sorry to tell you there's no change in the situation, sir. He's twice repeated his demand, and he refuses absolutely to extend the deadline."

Mulholland nodded, thoughts racing in all directions.

"But I want you to be in no doubt, no doubt whatsoever, that your safety, and the safety of the others, is what this operation is all about."

"Thank you."

"Everything else is—and will continue to be—subservient to that."

"Thank you."

"What I can't in any way estimate is how long Lander will stick it out, or what his further demands might be. We'll have to play those as and when they come; we've no option."

They were all grouped close, the way boxers and seconds listen to the referee before the opening bell.

"No heroics," O'Hare warned suddenly. "Don't try anything, whatever you do."

McConnell said: "And don't expect too much in the way of morale from the others. They were hit without warning and they've had a bad run."

"Right."

"D'you feel up to it?"

"I'm not exactly eager."

He managed a grim flicker of a smile, and McConnell marveled at his steadiness. "Will you come with me, please?"

All at once there was nothing more to be said. Mulholland found himself woodenly shaking hands with everybody. O'Hare gripped his arm; Ryder muttered "Wish it was me, Ralph," and somehow it registered that Ryder had never called him by his Christian name before. Briefly there was that element of disbelief again, and then a flutter in the guts to kill it dead.

"Bye," he said, countering with a touch of bravado. "See you."

He walked to the elevator with McConnell, just the two of them, and the doors slid across when McConnell stabbed the button. Neither spoke. Stone-faced they watched the indicator flash the floor numbers, then felt the drag as the braking slowed them.

Five . . . The number stayed lit, the doors pulled aside. "Turn left."

Three sharp paces took Mulholland into the angle by the stairs where Inspector Savage kept his vigil, and even as he moved there he saw the gaping doorways along the corridor and the armed SPG men and the scattered corn flakes to either side of the one door that remained closed. And suddenly nothing was the same any more; all morning had been leading him to this. Mulholland's heart picked up speed, and he felt the prickle of sweat among the hair stubble on the back of his neck.

"Anything, Bunny?" McConnell put to Savage.

"Not a whisper."

McConnell hesitated fractionally, then turned toward Mulholland. Their eyes met, and Mulholland's didn't waver. Brown eyes, flecked with green.

He said: "I guess this is about it, then. . . . Zero hour."

"Yes, sir."

McConnell checked with his watch. It was seconds short of five minutes to ten. He took the proffered bullhorn from Savage and began to warn Lander that the Ambassador was coming in.

"HE WILL KNOCK three times. . . . There will be three separate knocks—d'you hear me?"

Mulholland started to walk the forty or fifty paces separating him from 501, no before or after as he walked, only the claustrophobia of there and then. He passed the armed policemen wedged in the open doorway of 509, and the sense of abandonment was total, almost overpowering.

"Ralph!"

He turned in amazement. Unbelievably, Mary Kay was by the elevator, Savage and McConnell with their arms outstretched to restrain her. Mulholland's heart leaped. He had cut himself off and had been aware of nothing but the small carpeted sounds of his own making.

"I'll be here, Ralph. . . . All the time."

Something moved in him as never before. He raised a hand, in greeting and in farewell, all his love in the gesture, strength and resolution flowing from it. Then he squared his shoulders and turned away from her, certain in that moment that if he delayed he might weaken and perhaps find what he had to do impossible.

"The Ambassador will knock three times."

He reached the corn flakes and discarded cartons. Ten paces more to go. He steeled himself not to look back and he crunched across them, heralding his arrival. The splintered bullet hole in the door was chest high, its darkness like a secret observation place, and coldness brushed his nerves.

He halted with a final crunch, like snow underfoot, and gritted his teeth. Now . . . Three times he knocked, imagination beginning to rampage as he waited for a response, sweat oiling his face. Then he heard the lock turn and then the door swung inward.

The light was murky. For a second or two after he entered

he blinked, eyes adjusting. The girl was the first person he saw, Ireland a moment later. In the same instant the door was kicked shut behind him, and Mulholland swung carefully around, heel and toe, so as to face the man with the gun.

Incredibly, it wasn't Lander.

2

DAYLIGHT

10:00 A.M.

A TREMOR shook Mulholland. His jaw dropped and his mind seemed to make a deranged and convulsive lurch.

"*You!*"

"Get your jacket off."

He began to obey, stupefied. "What in the name of—"

"Empty out your trousers pockets."

Again he obeyed, beside himself with shock, faced with the strange intensity of a stare he vividly remembered.

"Listen, Grattan—"

"Shut your mouth."

"We thought you were Lander. . . . Everyone out there believes—"

"Shut it and sit down. On the bed."

Mulholland did as he was told, but slowly, like a man still tethered to the remnants of a dream. He had crammed himself with facts about Lander—background, education, service record, medical history, interests . . . all this and more. But to no purpose. Something had gone terribly wrong. The man with the gun was Grattan, Neil Grattan, until a month ago Mulholland's personal chauffeur.

He steadied himself, clammy tentacles of alarm reaching into his guts. Grattan wasn't normal; there was a bomb splinter lodged in his brain which impaired his visual memory. No driver worth employing could last with that kind of disability, and Grattan hadn't lasted. "I'm sorry, Grattan, but you'll have to go. . . ." The week after Easter, this was, the week in which he'd lost his way a score of different times, tempers frayed, appointments broken.

Mulholland said carefully: "What's this about, Grattan?"

No answer. The other two kept very still, and Mulholland spared them the briefest of glances, looking around him at the room's geography, the general disarray.

"You wanted me in here so we could talk."

"I wanted you in here, period."

Mulholland's jaw muscles quaked his cheeks. How could such a mistake have been made by those outside? The frantic thought once more possessed him. Everyone supposed they were dealing with Lander.

Knew it . . . They were that certain. And that wrong.

His jacket pockets were searched one-handed and the jacket was then tossed back at him. Grattan had positioned himself close to the door, hard against the wall there, a high-backed chair reversed between his legs, the rifle angled at forty-five degrees.

"How close are they in the corridor?"

Mulholland hesitated. "The nearest I saw was five, six doors away."

"Hand gun?"

"Yes."

"How many on this floor?" Grattan gestured angrily, delay unacceptable. "How many?" He spat it out.

"Half a dozen?"

"And elsewhere?"

"By the hundred," Mulholland said, and wondered what passed through Grattan's damaged and dangerous brain—a thought that scared him more than if he were at the mercy of a professional assassin.

Sweat stung the corners of his eyes. He glanced at the other two again, nervously as before, incredulity still with him, and saw what the last few hours had done to them. Ireland he vaguely recognized, the girl not at all. Both met his gaze, Gabrielle Wilding in hope of an ally, acknowledging his existence without words; but Ireland's eyes flicked hurriedly across to Grattan.

"I need a drink."

"Use the bathroom."

"Scotch."

"You've done too many commercials."

"For Christ's sake."

Grattan snorted and spoke to Mullholland. "We've an actor with us."

He stood up abruptly and crossed to the curtained windows, as quiet and jumpy as a cat, governed by some sort of plan. But what? What?

"Why me, Grattan?" Mulholland waited fractionally before risking it again. "Why me?"

"Who else but you?"

10:12 A.M.

DANNAHAY had been at the caravan for about three crowded minutes, and Llewellyn was coping as best he could.

"How many shots has he used?"

"Six."

119

"Any idea what his resources are?"

"No. But he's fired a couple of times as a warning, which would indicate he isn't short."

"Or could make him out to be plain jumpy."

"He's that, all right—reserves or no reserves."

"Worries me," Dannahay said.

After a night's near miss in another direction he wasn't too sure of himself. All at once he'd been expected to drop everything and switch his attention to a quite unprecedented situation. And a part of that situation didn't quite make sense. To others, maybe, but not to him; not yet, anyway.

Llewellyn frowned. "*What* worries you?" Dannahay was too damned laconic for his liking.

"Who's who, I guess."

And cryptic. "I don't understand."

"Nor the hell do I."

"You want their names again, you mean? The girl and the actor—is that it?"

"No."

"What, then?"

"Lander worries me." Dannahay squeezed his eyes as if a headache were coming on. "Give or take a man or two, he's about the least jumpy man I've met."

"Not any more. Something snapped in the night and sent him round the corner."

"I wouldn't bet on that."

The uneven murmur of the waiting reporters' voices rose and fell outside.

"Are you saying—"

"Not saying. Thinking."

"That's crazy. Absolutely crazy."

"Maybe, maybe not."

"Give me one good reason."

Dannahay measured him with a long look and thought:

No . . . Not on your life. But he said: "I'm not so strong on reasons, good ones least of all. On the other hand, s'far as hunches go—"

"A rifle's missing from his house."

"So I hear."

"And he was seen in Shelley's during the night."

"Uh-huh."

"Q.E.D." Llewellyn sucked in air. "God, it's two and two together."

"Seems like it, I admit." Dannahay nodded, then his mouth went slightly askew. "But addition's always been my weakness —you know how it is?"

"Look," Llewellyn said, impatient and skeptical. "Tell me just one thing."

"Sure."

"In the inconceivable event of it not being Lander, who you reckon could possibly be in there?"

"Ah," Dannahay said slowly. "Now that's an entirely different ball game."

10:16 A.M.

AFTERWARD Mary Kay Mulholland had no proper recollection of all the things she said and all the things she listened to Renata Lander say to her. They were using each other, drawing on each other's desperation in the hope somehow of mastering their own, though at the time it hadn't seemed like that.

"One thing I'm certain of," Mary Kay said, "is Ralph's ability to calm a situation . . . any situation."

"Harry wouldn't listen to us."

"Well, he's asked for Ralph, and we've got to build our hopes on that."

Noel was playing ticktacktoe with a constable sent to the room by McConnell, going through the motions, listening to every word. He kept glancing in their direction, sharing the strain, the waiting; no escape in the awful pretense of puzzling where a nought or a cross should go.

"I've prayed," Renata Lander said, bones showing white in the knuckles of her clenched hands. "I keep praying." She looked at the older woman, twenty years her senior. Last time they'd met had been at the Thanksgiving Day reception, something that seemed to belong to another existence. Already this one morning was everlasting.

"We're in the same boat, and we're going to have to ride—"

"But we aren't," Renata Lander exclaimed, suddenly swamped by a moment's violent envy. "We aren't, and you know it." Because of what had gone before, because of what would follow. "Who's *your* husband killed?"

Noel looked up sharply. Across the room she saw his stricken expression, and something more of her seemed to shrivel away.

"Oh Christ," she said to Mary Kay. "Oh Jesus Christ, forgive me," and reached to grasp her hands.

10:20 A.M.

"Helen?"

"Where are you?"

"Green Street," Roberto Olivares muttered out of a numbed mouth. "Phone booth."

"Why there, for Pete's sake?"

"Because I cannot get back. Because the idiots of police won't let me pass the barriers."

"Tell them who you are."

"No use."

"They don't believe."

Farce intruded even now. Helen Olivares lifted her eyes to the ceiling. The curlers were out of her hair at last, but nothing else had changed. She was working the switchboard still, normal calls as usual, a line kept open all the time to the room on the fifth closest to Savage's position, the greater part of her attention concentrated on the signal light of 501.

"Which barrier were you at?"

"Lees Place." His tongue seemed to be out of control. "Lees Place and Park Street."

"Go back there and wait."

"No good, I tell you."

"Go back there and wait." She was sharper than she knew. "I'll get word to them."

"Very well." Then: "I had it out, Helen."

One day they'd laugh at this; but not now, God not now. "Make it soon, will you? There's a hotel grinding to a halt around me here every minute you're away."

A fly buzzed frenetically against the window, trapped in the sunlight behind the drawn curtains, and they listened to it, all of them, the sound drilling into their minds.

Mulholland sat with his thick arms folded, not moving, still shaken by what he had found. He wanted to tell the others who Grattan really was; it seemed important. He wanted them to know that Grattan had come to him as his personal chauffeur just six months ago after discharge from the British Army, nothing apparently wrong with him, references impeccable, wounded in Belfast the year before, the discharge an honorable one, no fault to find.

Until, that is, he reported for duty and the bewildering shortness of his visual memory was exposed.

To begin with, the lapses were unaccountable—the Embassy passed by as if it didn't exist, Mary Kay ignored and left standing at the Dorchester, the Cenotaph unrecognized. "Here, sir? . . . Here, sir?"—he was forever asking, forever peering around. Everywhere and everyone seemed strange to him; new. And not just the first time; over and over. Mulholland began by suspecting nerves, then drink, then drugs. When challenged, Grattan admitted to a sliver of metal buried inoperably in his brain, the effect of which was partially to erase the images that would normally be stored. A few hours, a night's sleep, and he was left with at best a blur to match against what his eyes were then seeing.

Despite this, despite the difficulties, they had persevered with him, Mary Kay more patient than Mulholland. Grattan's other senses came to his aid, and he used them to compensate the way the blind do. He didn't spare himself. Some days were better than others, and no one would have guessed he had a problem. But gradually the work became too much for him. After a few weeks he began to crack—sweating at the wheel, muttering, nostrils flared; it was pitiful. And embarrassing. And increasingly intolerable. Twice in the same day he couldn't find his way back to Winfield House. And he changed as the pressure mounted, growing surly, sometimes erupting with unexplained rage, hastening the inevitable end—"I'm sorry, Grattan, but you'll have to go. . . ."

All this Mulholland recalled, a succession of vivid cameos printed on his inner eye as he watched Grattan now, ten feet away, and heard the fly buzz and bump against the glass in the dead-air silence of the room.

"Whose gun've you got there, Grattan? Is it Lander's? Harry Lander's?" No one else was going to tell him how the mistake was born. "Is that how they've put him into your shoes?"

"Cut it out," Grattan raged. "Cut it out, d'you hear?"

10:32 A.M.

LANDER came out of the midmorning coolness of Victoria Station and picked up a taxi right away. MAYFAIR SIEGE—LATEST; he noticed the posters but the message didn't bite. The clothes he wore were the clothes he'd worn last night, but they were tired-looking now, the shirt collar limp and the shoes dirt-stained.

"Bruton Mews."

He yawned and stroked his jawbone, back-of-the-hand. The hair on his head was thick and straight and dark, no sign of thinning anywhere, no sign of anything much about him except tiredness. A baggy softness under the brown eyes, perhaps; two fingers dyed with nicotine. He was just short of good-looking, very compact, tapering from the shoulders to a narrow waist. His passport had him on record at five feet ten, and much of the time he weighed around one hundred and seventy pounds, but none of this mattered at the moment. The important thing was getting back home and picking up the pieces.

Once again.

And he dreaded it, uneasy despite the fatigue, uneasy in more ways than he could ever speak of, on the rack with wondering how everything would end.

Where'd he been? *Walking* . . . All night? *Yes, all night* . . . For ten hours? *Why not?* . . . But that's ridiculous. *Is it?* . . . Where? Where'd he been walking? . . . And so on, and so on. Hundred to one that's the way it would go.

He closed his eyes and let the blood-red darkness in, feeling the centrifugal drag on his body as the taxi wheeled at Hyde Park Corner. Noel would be at school, so there'd only be the two of them. But it couldn't last indefinitely; he was as late as hell for work as it was. So they'd leave it unfinished and start all over tonight.

Eastbourne? He'd thumbed a ride to Eastbourne? *Because that's where the guy happened to be going* . . .

They arrived at Bruton Mews via Piccadilly and Berkeley Square, the traffic flow normal, the pavements thronged, no hint along the way of what awaited him. Even when they made the final turn and Lander saw the solitary policeman he didn't connect him with himself. He got out and paid his fare, glancing up at the house, apprehensive in a quite different fashion. Only as he started toward the door did the policeman intercept him.

"Sorry, sir, but I'll have to ask you your business."

"Business?" A warning prickle on the back of his neck. "How d'you mean, business?"

"What's the purpose of your visit, sir?" The press and God knows who had been as thick as flies all morning. "You *are* wanting Number 14?"

"I live here," Lander said.

"Oh yes?" The constable was trained to doubt and disbelieve, if possible to be polite. "May I have your name, please?"

"Lander . . . Harry Lander."

In all his life he'd never seen a man's expression change so abruptly.

A car was there within minutes. McConnell was too professional for his consternation to show, but he was in the grip of it, wanting the evidence of his own eyes before rejecting the possibility of a hoax.

"Mr. Lander?" Embassy pass, driving license, credit cards— he flipped them through. "What's your wife's name, Mr. Lander? . . . How many children've you got? . . . Are you in possession of the keys of this house?" The day would hardly pass without its cranks and sensation seekers, but this wasn't one of them. This was Lander, all right, H. R. Lander, and there were questions screaming to be answered, red-faced explaining to be done. "Get in, Mr. Lander."

"Listen," Lander began shakily. "There's a lot I want to know, a whole lot—"

"On the way."

"Where we going?"

"Shelley's."

"You mean to say I'm believed to be in there?" He started on what the constable had dazed him with, as if the repetition might somehow turn it into lies. "Me?"

"That's right."

"With a rifle?"

"That's right."

"And Ralph Mulholland taken as a hostage?"

"That's right."

"*Me?*"

They left Berkeley Square behind, tires snickering through the turn.

"We had our reasons," McConnell said brusquely. "Good ones."

"I'm supposed to've killed a man—yes?"

"Someone has."

"You pinned it on me, though. You've pinned the whole of whatever's been happening—"

"We had our reasons."

"*Wow!*" Lander fumbled for cigarettes, anger glinting in his eyes. "Somebody's going to have to answer for this."

"We'll get around to that. Meanwhile, keep the facts in mind." McConnell listed them. "They're what we had to go on—and they clearly pointed to you. Everything pointed to you, your absence included."

"Where's my wife?"

"At Shelley's." They were almost at the hotel now. "Your son's there too."

Lander glanced sidelong at McConnell with a look of bitter hurt, something else dawning. He seemed to be coming to terms with everything piecemeal. "How long've they been caught up in this?"

"Three hours?" McConnell suggested. "I'm sorry," he then said, "but I had no choice."

"What did she tell you?"

"Enough."

"More facts?" Scorn in the tone.

"I'll say this," McConnell told him evenly. "She and your boy dug their toes in over you. They've never gone along with our conclusions, not in their hearts. Isn't that good for you to know?"

"Mr. Lander, please . . . Mr. Lander . . . Over here, Harry . . ."

Word had preceded them, and they couldn't escape the photographers or the jostling or the excited clash of voices.

"Damn them," McConnell muttered as the elevator doors sealed them in. "Damn them all."

They rode up together to the fifth and the silence waiting for them there, hardly a movement from the positioned sharp-shooters, the tension electric, only one thing any different for McConnell—and this an unknown quantity, nothing to go on.

He led Lander along the length of the corridor in the other direction, signaled him to wait, and went without hesitation into the end room. Lander paused, looking back at Savage's men, wondering what had been done in his name, appalled and resentful; and uneasy, no time to weigh the damage.

"Harry?"

He turned to find Renata in the doorway, a fever in her eyes of incredulous relief. Noel was with her, pale beyond words, a seeming slow motion about the way he started toward him with his arms outspread, almost taking him off his feet, laughing, sobbing, clinging.

"Whoa," Lander said, emotions torn in half. "Hey, there . . ."

McConnell left them to it. He owed them this—and more, much more. Pity was an incurable disease, but there were hard practical things to be done and he couldn't afford to be moved. He re-entered the room where Mary Kay Mulholland was now alone with the uniformed constable. A minute earlier he had gone straight over to Renata Lander and whispered the heart-stopping news—"Hang on to yourself, take it easy"— Noel close enough to pick it up and stiffen and begin to move. This second time he paused halfway across to where Mary Kay stood by the window.

"I heard," she said, and he nodded as if he'd been accused. "And I'm . . . I'm glad for them." Anxiety hard held, choked back. "So very glad." Her dignity was enormous, and humbling, but her eyes were asking every question he was asking himself.

"We've had our wires crossed, Mrs. Mulholland."

"What happens now?"

"We play it as it comes—same as before. And go to work on what we thought we knew."

10:56 A.M.

"PHIL?"

"Every time," Richard Ireland's agent said.

"I'm being pestered by a character by the name of Kent, does features for the *Star*. S'far as I can pin him down, he's intending putting a piece together on the way he reckons Ireland's making out."

"Balls."

"The way the public sees him. In character."

"Balls."

"He's very persuasive, Phil. Argues it'll do Richard and the series a whole lot of good, particularly if he can style it the way he's got in mind. Part fact, part fantasy."

"It stinks."

"Kent's asking for as much background as I can give him, but I thought I'd check with you first."

"It stinks," Phil repeated. "I hate it. And you ought to hate it too, every rotten part of it."

"Whether I hate it or not, he's going ahead. I can't stop him. Every reporter within a mile of Grosvenor Square's scrambling for something different, and this is what Kent's going for. No good me tut-tutting and waving a finger in his face; he's going to do it, Phil. Like it or not."

"Then he ought to be shot. A thing like that—God, you ought to be telling him to go sod himself instead of—"

"Listen, Phil."

"You bloody listen." A radio was on his desk, and the next news came at the top of the hour. "We're talking 'bout something real, for Christ's sake. Real people, and a real sweaty situation, and real life or real death in the balance." He took a sharp intake of breath before slamming the receiver down. "Sometimes I reckon you people don't know what the word means."

11:16 A.M.

SOMEWHERE in the distance, on the very edge of earshot, an ambulance siren linked them briefly to the outside world.

Mulholland rested his elbows on his knees, leaning forward, Ireland to one side of him, the girl to the other. Silence he found demoralizing, and potentially dangerous; Grattan's unease seemed to feed on it.

With as much calm as he could summon he said: "You feel you've got a grievance with me—okay; I accept that. But what've you got against these other two?"

"Nothing."

"That's good to hear." Mulholland delayed, ultracautious, no means of telling what the man's expression meant. "They've served their purpose, so why not let them go?"

"That's for me to decide."

"How about the young lady? Just her, say? Losing her won't weaken your hand."

"I decide. Who, when, how, what—*I* decide. Nobody else."

"Sure."

Mulholland dropped his gaze. The only way McConnell could discover who he was dealing with was for one of them to be released. So he must keep at it, hinting, water on a stone.

"You tired?" McConnell said to Helen Olivares.

"Yes and no."

"Can you stay at the board?"

"As long as you want me."

"The girl knows your voice, and so does he. So you're reassuring to them both—and with him especially that's important. A change now might trigger God knows what."

"I'm good for hours yet."

"Fine." McConnell slipped a peppermint into his mouth. "Call the room, will you?" The bullhorn was too impersonal, one-way traffic. "Let's have another try."

"What do I say?"

"Ask him what his intentions are. Now he's got the Ambassador ask him what more he wants."

She rang through. McConnell listened on the extension as she spoke, the man's refusal to be drawn no more than a staccato murmur in the background.

"Remind him of this." Once again he applied the screw as best he could by way of Helen Olivares and Gabrielle Wilding: but he was talking to a stranger now, every word a gesture in the dark. "We can wait all day, all day and all night. Hell, he's a sensible man, so he must know the odds. However long he drags this out, we can outlast him. So why not make a move and quit? Now, while it's easy and we're still talking with each other?"

To his surprise he drew a reply. "He says he'll make a move when daylight's gone, and not before."

11:34 A.M.
DANNAHAY offered Lander a cigarette and began feeling for a lighter, tapping his pockets. "Shouldn't have happened to a dog. Never known anything like it, not anywhere."

"I want to see Ryder about the whole lousy business."

"You bet."

"It's intolerable my wife and son should have been subjected to what they've had to go through. . . . Monstrous."

"I go along with that. If it'd been me, I'd raise the roof." Dannahay lit up and blew smoke. They were in the men's room on the ground floor at Shelley's, and Dannahay had sidetracked Lander there the moment the elevator brought him down. "Listen, Harry. Won't keep you more'n a minute, but I've been assigned to liaise with the British, and one of the areas I'm concerned with is what you did with yourself last night."

"How d'you mean?"

"Where you went."

"Oh, that," Lander said sharply. "That's Renata's territory."

"Want a rehearsal?"

"What's the point?"

"They figure someone got into your place and lifted your rifle—right? And your jacket—right? More besides, for all I know—right?"

"So I'm told."

"Clear as glass now you've showed. They're checking for fingerprints and all, and the theory is the guy knows you *and* Mulholland. Both. Which sort of narrows the field."

"I've had their theories," Lander said, tired and drawn and unlikely to forgive. "Christ, when I think—"

"Sure, sure," Dannahay agreed sympathetically. "Everyone's been arse upward until an hour ago, and you're right to beef. But so as I can kind of get the whys and wherefores all together I'd appreciate your telling me where you took off to in such a hurry."

"Eastbourne."

"How'd you get down there?"

"Thumbed a ride in Park Lane. Could easily have been Brighton—or wherever. I wasn't aiming anywhere special."

"What time was that? . . . Sort of."

"After midnight."

"How'd you come back? Train?"

Lander nodded.

"Didn't see a paper? Hear the radio?"

"No."

"Sure would have helped if you had. Sure would have helped everyone, specially Mulholland. He went in stone dead certain it was you. I reckon it influenced him—you know that?" Dannahay snorted. "Crazy, isn't it? What's worse than being wise after the event?"

Lander said: "I'll have to go, John. They're waiting for me."

"First I'll tell you one more thing."

"Okay."

"Sounds smart and all, but I never went along with the pack. Not really. I never properly swallowed it, right from the time I heard." Dannahay hollowed his cheeks as he inhaled. "It just isn't your style, Harry."

"Thanks," Lander said. "Thanks a lot."

11:50 A.M.

WHEN IRELAND heard Grattan tell the girl about waiting until dark, he started to shiver. Fear bred a sickness all its own, and fear had made him empty, left no reserves, none of the inner strength the others seemed able to claw out of themselves. He clenched his teeth and felt the shivering rake his body and tried not to look at Grattan.

Night was hours from now, and in panic he told himself that none of them would survive that long. All morning Grattan had never been more than a heartbeat away from using the gun, and at any moment something in him could snap again—nothing to lose, men shot already.

What did he want with them, on and on? . . . The sense of panic flooded higher in Ireland's mind. When he glanced at Gabrielle Wilding and saw the contempt behind her scared veneer, he didn't care, past caring, the naked feel of her forgotten, the vanities of his own virility forgotten, the person he'd always assumed he was forgotten.

He shivered, at the mercy of every move Grattan made, everything he said, every change of tone. He'd never make it through to nightfall. He didn't know about the others, and he didn't care. But he cared about himself, and he knew all too well that he was breaking under the strain—and was powerless to stop it.

If anyone went out of here, it had to be him. *Had to be . . .*

Deep within himself he noticed Mulholland nod in his direction. "Mind if I speak to him?" This to Grattan, Mulholland taking the risk. "Something I remember."

"Remember what?" The eyes shuttered, then stared, restless and suspicious.

Mulholland faced toward Ireland. "Seems an odd time to be telling you, but my wife and I saw you on television a couple of weeks ago and we both got a great deal of pleasure from your performance." Very courageous, calculated, the shivering ignored. "'A Walk in the Park'—wasn't that the one?" He even smiled, part of the rescue attempt.

"You cut that out," Grattan barked, with his hard-to-place accent.

"Where's the harm?"

"I do the talking."

Mulholland shrugged and spread his hands. "You used to be a great TV man."

"Lay off, d'you hear?" The stare was wild again.

"Okay, if you insist. But I had it in mind—"

"*For Christ's sake*," Ireland pleaded. "*Stop it, can't you?*"

"Sure." There was a second or two's silence, but Mulholland wouldn't let go. "I've got an advantage over you two." He was stretching Grattan as far as he dared. "Mr. Grattan and I have known each other for quite some while, so it's natural I should want to speak with him. The silences are hell, let's face it. And I reckon having the four of us cooped up in here together is bad on all our nerves. It's certainly bad on mine."

Sweat was dribbling coldly down his spine. He kept his eyes on the gun and risked one more thing.

"When're you going to thin us out, Grattan? When're you going to let these people go?"

12:07 P.M.

HELEN OLIVARES looked up at her husband, that moment arrived. "You made it, then?"

". . . something awful." He muttered out of one side of his mouth, handkerchief pressed close. "Nothing but trouble."

"You'll survive," she said briskly. "Now, first, we've got reservation and accommodation problems along the entire fifth floor—"

"I'm bleeding, Helen."

"*What?*"

"I'm bleeding bad. I've got to lie down somewhere quick."

God in heaven, she thought, and watched him lurch away.

———

Lander said: "But I *had* a jacket. When I went out of here I was wearing a suit—*this* one." He was on his third Scotch already. "So why should I want to come back in for something more to wear?"

"It made sense at the time . . . terrible sense." Renata Lander tossed her dark hair. "When I found the rifle gone, that did it for me. I was so screwed up I can't recall too much, but I do remember calling Jackman. . . . I was pretty frantic, Harry, desperate, and what with the gun gone and the ten pounds taken—you know?—and the rest of it . . ."

She let a gesture finish for her. Twice within the last four hours she had been taken apart enough for any one lifetime. Half an hour ago the three of them had struggled back to Bruton Mews through inevitable crowds. And here, among the chintzes in the room where her own ordeal had begun, she had held Harry Lander close and tight and asked forgiveness and laughed a little hysterically; and wondered, even as she did so, whether anything could be quite the same between them ever again.

He pulled the edge of the curtain aside and gazed resentfully at the knot of people gathered in the mews. Sharp and bitter he said: "Have a row with your wife and get yourself branded as a killer. How about that? . . . Instant fame. Every damned stone turned over for all to see." He drank. "How long're we going to be the center of attraction?"

"The center of attraction's over at Shelley's, Harry. . . . This won't last."

"No? Listen. I'll always be the guy who was believed to have run amok. Live that one down. If they thought me capable of it once, they'll think me capable of it again. Next month, next year—someone'll always gawk and say—"

"Nonsense, Harry."

"Stands to reason."

Renata Lander measured her words. "Everything's been

answered for Noel and me—prayers, wishes, hopes . . . everything. What we hung onto's come true." She wiped her bruised eyes. "So for me—and I guess for Noel too—every single person waiting in the mews right now is a part of the miracle. I dread to think how it would be if they weren't there; what it would mean. . . . Don't you see, Harry?"

He didn't seem to have listened. "What gets me is the way the police make a scapegoat of you and then backpedal. It hasn't taken them long to find out how and where the house was busted into. So why couldn't they have had the sense to come up with that before now? Hell, a man doesn't break into his own house."

"I've known it to happen."

"Even so." He drained the glass. "I need a shave," he said, "and a shower."

He was on his way, loosening his tie, when she spoke from across the room. "Harry."

"Yeah?"

"I love you, Harry. . . . You've no idea."

He nodded, flushed in the face now, a gloss on his eyes from the whisky.

"Well, then . . . No more giving chance a chance—okay?"

Her lips trembled. "Never again?"

"Okay," he said.

The telephone rang. Both started toward it, but Lander was there first.

"Harry?"

"Speaking." He covered the mouthpiece and said to Renata: "Ryder." For a short while he listened, one eyebrow raised. Then he cut in: "Yes, well there's a whole lot I have to say about that myself. It seems to me I've been the subject of outright character assassination, for one thing, while my family's been caused dreadful distress. . . . Right. Yes, I know. . . . And I certainly want to see *you*." He glanced at his watch. "Three quarters of an hour will suit me fine. Sure . . . G'bye, then."

He hung up, nursing the mood. "You going out?"

"Yes." She nodded.

"See that Noel makes school, will you?" He began peeling off his jacket. "The sooner he's back to normal the better it'll be for him." Normality seemed an obsession with him, as if the drama at Shelley's was a continuing reflection on himself. "What're you doing?"

"I'm going over to the hotel," Renata Lander said. "I want to be with Mary Kay Mulholland."

12:18 P.M.

WHEN THE KEY gritted in the lock, Joan Knollenberg couldn't believe her ears.

"Charles? . . . Charles?"

"It'd better be," he said, coming in.

"What's going on?"

"Got leave of absence."

"You kidding?" She had a little tinsel laugh and a turned-up nose and wet-look lips. "How d'you mean? You been fired, or something?"

"Not yet," he said, humming a few bars. "I just got nothing much to do for a while. I'm sort of odd man out, honey."

"Since when?"

"Since John Dannahay dropped everything in favor of Mulholland."

"Ah." She had kissed him when he arrived, and she was only just beginning to realize he hadn't let her go. "Is John in charge of what they're trying to do over there?"

"Not exactly."

"It's bad, isn't it? Ugly . . . I been listening. Ralph Mulholland's such a sweet man." He had started to unbutton her blouse, and she seemed taken unawares. "Hey!"

"Haven't seen you for days, honey. Been keeping all the wrong hours, remember?"

"You ought to give a girl some warning." She struggled a little, not very hard. "'Nother thing—I've only just done my hair."

"Aw, come on." He grinned, inches away. "How long've we been married?"

"Four years."

"And who wins?"

"You win." Eyes all sultry.

"So?" he said.

"Charlie Knollenberg, you're a devil."

Later, some time later, she said: "Just what have you and Dannahay been digging into these past weeks?"

"That'd be telling, wouldn't it?"

"Doesn't matter to me."

Knollenberg allowed himself a rare disclosure. "Let's just say that one of our people's been misbehaving himself."

"Like this?"

"Not like this," he said. "Not like this at all."

12:35 P.M.

"Yes, sir." The Commissioner of Police ran his free hand over the smooth dome of his bald head. "Yes, indeed . . . Irrespective of the gunman's identity. It's been a waiting game from the first, and it will stay that way until he shows his hand. Sooner or later, sir, he's going to make fresh demands or want to do a deal or decide to move out. Until then we really have no option but to sit tight and keep him contained."

This was the second time within the hour that the Home

Secretary had telephoned, anxious as ever, due at Downing Street in exactly ten minutes from now and making certain he was briefed.

"Nothing's changed," the Commissioner told him, "except for the elimination of the man Lander as a suspect. The alternative open to Chief Superintendent McConnell is to rush the room where the hostages are held, but only in the very last resort would this be seriously considered. With or without the use of gas, McConnell is of the opinion that casualties would be inevitable, and he's not prepared to run that kind of risk until such time as he has absolutely no other choice— a view I strongly endorse. . . ."

The Commissioner frowned. "Sorry, sir—what was that? . . . Oh yes, every confidence. I'd rather McConnell was dealing with this than anyone I know."

"This is Shelley's Hotel, situated in the Mayfair district of London, England, and a proverbial stone's throw from the American Embassy. From the fire escape of this hotel, at around dawn local time today, an as-yet-unknown gunman shot and killed an as-yet-unknown vagrant some hundred and fifty yards away on the edge of Grosvenor Square. . . ."

CBS television was in possession of the corner of Fairfield Walk, which a BBC crew had just vacated.

"Shortly after this apparently motiveless killing, the gunman entered a bedroom on the fifth floor here and took a man and woman hostage. At six o'clock there was further shooting, during which a uniformed policeman was wounded. A little over two hours later the gunman demanded that Ralph Mulholland, American Ambassador to the Court of St. James's, come in to join the other hostages. . . ."

The camera felt its way over the oblique face of the hotel. Despite the narrow angle, it was a safe position from which to film, and much in demand. You could illustrate the prob-

lems, the closeness of everything, the impregnability of the
floor in question. A reporter could stand here and say his
piece.

"For a considerable period earlier this morning it was believed that the gunman was himself an American employed
at the Embassy. But the British authorities have recently
admitted they were in error on this point, and the mystery of
the gunman's identity remains. Contact with him has been
intermittent, and since the Ambassador joined the other
hostages it has all but ceased.

"Inside Shelley's, and at vantage points elsewhere, police
marksmen are deployed in strength. All activity in the block
in which the hotel is situated has come to a virtual standstill.
Close by, on all sides, noonday life in the metropolis goes on
undisturbed and unrestricted. But here the atmosphere is
tense in the extreme, the immediate quiet almost uncanny.
Here we are witnessing a war of nerves, a war that everyone
knows cannot last forever—not least the man with the
gun. . . ."

McConnell wasn't quite certain about Dannahay; once before, they'd worked together, and to this day he hadn't been
able to make up his mind about him. Shrewd, certainly; quick
and inventive and thorough. But whether he liked him was
another matter. Cold fish.

"You people pick up any fingerprints at the Lander house?"

"Too many."

Dannahay grunted. "Too many can be almost worse than
none at all."

"They're working on them," McConnell said.

"You go along with my view that the guy knew Lander
kept a gun?"

"Very much. But I'm not so sure he's taken Mulholland for
any other reason than that the American Ambassador's al-

most the best lever he could lay his hands on. Short of the Queen, and most of the Royals, there's no one around to touch Mulholland."

"You're figuring he wants to open a fair-sized can of worms—right?"

"Could be," McConnell muttered, doubting his own judgment after what had happened. "I'm not saying he and the Ambassador are strangers to each other; not necessarily. But I *am* saying that whereas he must have raided Bruton Mews because he knew what was there, he doesn't need to be acquainted with the Ambassador to appreciate his value."

"Either way," Dannahay said, dusting ash from his lapels, "it's early in the game yet. He's given plenty of notice about his intentions."

"Damn all use we can make of it—unless, that is, we can get the girl out. Or the actor, say; one or the other. We'd have most of the answers then. . . . But I'm not making any more approaches. It's stony ground, and dangerous. He's as jumpy as hell, for one thing, so I'm continuing to maintain as low a profile as possible until he decides to contact us. Then, maybe, I can try some bargaining. Meanwhile we go on with the waiting—and I'm beginning to think it's about the hardest thing I know."

"It's good for ulcers," Dannahay said. "That's for sure."

12:52 P.M.

THERE WAS television in the waiting room, black-and-white, the picture in need of adjustment, but as far as Sergeant Dysart was concerned the focus distortion didn't matter. He was waiting for the ward sister to say when he could go in to see Yorke and he wasn't watching with more than half an eye. Only when the latest Czarina Vodka commercial ran its brief course did his interest sharpen.

"She will come to you cold," Richard Ireland assured him, using the silky Nick Sudden voice as a fur-clad beauty approached, "but soon she will set you afire. And in the morning it will seem such a *harmless* pleasure." A fluttered eyelid, not quite a wink, from a departing troika. "That's . . . the miracle of your Czarina."

Unknown to Dysart, the sister was behind his chair; somehow he'd missed the starchy rustle. "Strange, isn't it," she said, "to see that and yet to know where he is, and to wonder what he must be going through? Sort of weird . . . I think he's gorgeous."

Dysart stood up. "Can I go in now?"

"Don't stay too long."

"I won't."

"His mother and father are with him."

It was a smallish ward, perhaps a dozen beds, Yorke at the far end on the left. Dysart walked on tiptoe, nodding self-consciously at other patients he passed. Yorke's middle-aged parents were sitting on either side of the bed, though at the start he scarcely noticed them.

"Hallo." Four hours he'd waited. "How's it going, then? All right?"

"Fine." Only a whisper, but good to hear.

"They tell me you're going to be like new."

"Sure."

"Known people go to extremes before, but this is ridiculous." Dysart grinned at the bloodless face propped on the pillow. "What a way to chicken out of a best-man speech."

"Bananas," Yorke breathed, and winced as he tried to join in the laughter.

GRATTAN stiffened suddenly and rose from the chair like a man slowly rising in his stirrups. Three paces brought him crabwise along the wall to the door. He listened there, head cocked, eyes slitted with suspicion yet never once unwatchful, the mark of the soldier in the way he moved and held the gun, the look of a madman in the set of his face, unnerving the way he peered as if constantly renewing his impression of them.

False alarm . . . He armed sweat from his forehead, lamplight and daylight diffused in the room.

"They'd never chance it." He chose Gabrielle Wilding. "Know that?" She looked away and his anger flared. "*Know that?*"

"Yes."

"When I speak to you, you answer."

"Yes."

"They'd never chance it, I tell you." Nerves transferred him to Mulholland. "Who's got the most cards to play? Them or me?"

"I couldn't say."

"No?" It was like a threat.

Mulholland took a little time, thinking, thinking. "I can't say because I don't know what you're going for."

"Plenty."

"Of course." He still had a hope that he might gain Grattan's confidence, somehow break him down. "But what?"

"I'll come to that when I'm good and ready."

"It won't be dark till nine." Mulholland glanced at his watch. "What're you after besides a safe passage?"

An unstable smile twisted Grattan's features, but he held his tongue. And the smile vanished, cunning taking over. Everyone was quiet then, the silence eating away at them, at

Ireland most of all, a little less of them left the longer they endured.

Inspector Savage had changed his men in the key positions, relieving some, switching others. There was a limit to the time they could stay at peak alertness, and alertness was all; in the end the merest part of a second could decide.

"What I can't fathom," he muttered to McConnell, just arrived by elevator, "is why he loosed off at a harmless old bum in the first place."

"Draw attention to himself?"

"If he knew where the rifle was, then I reckon the whole shebang's premeditated."

"We only *think* he knew, Bunny."

Savage nodded along the corridor at the one closed door and its warning mat of breakfast cereal. Their voices were right down. "You saying this is all an impulse thing?"

"Some of it," McConnell said, weary of guesswork. "The killing possibly. Mulholland no. He intended to get Mulholland."

"Why the one and then the other? They don't tie up."

"Are you suggesting there's a book of rules?" The pressures on McConnell were beginning to show. "How the hell do I know a single why or a single how if none of us even has a glimmer who we're dealing with?"

Impotence and exasperation propelled him across the corridor into the room where the house-phone link with the switchboard was maintained.

"Anything?" he snapped.

"No, sir," the constable said.

Of course there wasn't anything. He'd have known.

1:18 P.M.

GRATTAN flipped finger and thumb at Gabrielle Wilding. "Tell 'em we want food."

She hesitated. Mulholland caught her searching eye and nodded.

"Sandwiches and coffee, plenty of both. And tell 'em how we want it delivered—same as before. . . . Exactly the same as before."

"We," he'd said. . . . She got up and went to the telephone. And all at once she was shaking. She hadn't expected a second chance.

O'Hare had come with cognac and cigarettes, and he was urging Mary Kay to move.

"One floor down," he told her, "there's a vacant suite. Far more suitable. Wouldn't you consider it?"

"No."

"This place isn't cut out for waiting in." Renata Lander was there as well, sharing the vigil, keeping silence at bay with distractions about children, family, home; all that. O'Hare looked at the two women and at what the bedroom had in the way of furniture and thought how much more comfortable they could be. "Don't you think, in the circumstances . . . ?"

"No." Mary Kay was quiet but firm. "I want to be here, close as possible, and that's that. . . . Thanks, Sam, all the same."

"You're the boss," he said.

He had to hand it to her; she was very, very solid. Typical Mulholland.

146

"How much longer?"

"A minute or two," Helen Olivares answered, quick as a knife. "Tell him that. . . . Two minutes and a tray'll be on its way."

Grattan heard. "High time," he said, the endless threat sustained. "High bloody time."

He gestured, indicating to Gabrielle Wilding she was to hang up, and she obeyed, avoiding his gaze yet feeling the burning weight of it. An aircraft was passing overhead, not loud but clearly audible, and the sound filled her with a trembling surge of envy for anyone who was free. All she could think of now was opening the door again and stepping outside.

"When the food's delivered, you go get it," he said. "Same way as before."

Woodenly she nodded, afraid lest she betrayed herself.

"And you come back in the same as before." It was as if he had read her thoughts. "You'll hate yourself forever if you don't."

A tiny fraction of the day went by, the throb of the aircraft receding. Mulholland bent to fasten a shoe, and she followed the movement, edgy, everything near the nerve.

"Understood?"

Mulholland flashed her a glance. Go, it said. Go if you can.

"Understood?" Grattan bullied.

She nodded, a pendulum swinging, Ireland still a part of the choice, like it or not.

"Say it, then."

Go . . . Mulholland's private signals were conveyed in a fraction of a second's intensity, crystal clear. *Grab the chance.*

"Say you understand."

"I understand," Gabrielle Wilding said, and felt her heart thud against her ribs.

They sat and waited, silence back again, time marking time, a freak of memory inexplicably reminding Mulholland that he was to have been at a charity luncheon at the Hilton— he and Mary Kay. He shut his mind to it, another world out there, willing the girl not to falter, telling himself he believed he could handle Grattan.

She started visibly when the telephone rang. Grattan rose with the rifle leveled at his hip, watching as she lifted the receiver.

"The food is with you."

He motioned her toward the door, with its tuft of pink toilet paper rammed into the splintered hole in the woodwork. He was against the wall now, confident, the others covered. Ireland was on the rim of her vision, but she didn't look at him, an awful indecision turning to panic.

"Get on out." He moved the gun.

And stay out, Mulholland's message read.

She reached for the bolt and slid it across, the thud a warning to those outside: she thought of that. Seconds later she pulled the door wide open, delaying before stepping into the corridor, greeted by the same breathless quiet. Then she walked, slowly at first, crunching through the cereal on high heels, the tray placed where the scatter ended.

She was strangely rigid as she walked; all his life Savage was to remember how terrified she was as she started toward him. The nearest police marksman partially broke cover, mouthing as before "Come on, come *on*"—motioning urgently, a narrow-faced man in grey. The look of him registered with her as well as his actions—the sandwiches too, white bread and brown—all of it recorded in cold-sweat seconds, drawn out, a pounding in her ears, same as the last time.

Yet not the same.

When she came level with the tray all the stiffness left her. Suddenly. She ran, mouth open, arms wide, twenty, thirty paces, and Savage grabbed her, pulling her into where he was.

Moments afterward the door of 501 crashed shut. From inside there came a bawling, crying noise and the sound of breaking. And Gabrielle Wilding listened in dread, cringing as she panted in Savage's arms.

1:44 P.M.

"GRATTAN . . . Says the name's Grattan."

"*Grattan?*"

"Seems to have knowledge of Mulholland. That's what she says."

"Check with the Embassy, will you? Try Osborne . . . Try Dannahay."

"Grattan?" Dannahay queried, and paused, forehead puckered. Then he closed his eyes and groaned. "Grattan . . ." Never so much as given him a thought. "Grattan," he repeated, still trying the name for sense. Hindsight had a stinking habit of cutting you down to size. "Sure, sure . . . Grattan, yes. But how's it come about nobody even hooked the smallest of question marks against that guy, for Chrissake?"

When Gabrielle Wilding broke into a run and they heard the sound of it and knew she had gone, a bout of madness engulfed Grattan. He shouted as he booted the door to, and then he began to break everything he could use the rifle on, snarling and whining as he did so.

Mulholland backed away to the wall and flattened, motionless: Ireland cowered at the foot of the bed. Grattan lurched about the room, sledge-hammering the rifle butt against pictures and mirrors, hurling aside lamps and ashtrays, kicking the furniture, his strength and viciousness terrifying. If the other two had been prepared, and in unison, they might have been able to tackle him, but though for brief moments he was vulnerable, the chances went begging.

Mulholland flinched as the Nolan prints on either side of his head were sent crashing to the floor. Ireland scrambled to the bathroom and locked himself in. God knows how long Mulholland stood alone, hands and teeth clenched, in fear of his life as never before, praying for the storm to die.

Whole minutes must have passed before the destruction came to an end, by which time the room was a shambles. Grattan's final act of fury was to smash the ceiling light. He was half sobbing by then, no less dangerous but more easily observed and measured. And in the slightly increased gloom Mulholland noticed that the telephone remained untouched— almost as if one area of Grattan's mind had never quite gone into the frenzy.

1:50 P.M.
"GRATTAN?" Mary Kay was on her feet. "Of course, of course . . ." It seemed to take time to sink in. She looked over at Renata Lander. "Grattan . . . Ralph's onetime driver. The one who was sick." Then she wheeled on McConnell, there with the news. "But *why?* Just because Ralph couldn't use him any more?"

Kent was in the foyer when Gabrielle Wilding was escorted down in the elevator, a car waiting for her at the hotel's rear, the immediate questioning done but more to follow.
"Miss Wilding . . ."
He was a jump ahead of the rest. Since dawn he'd drawn blanks, nothing out of the ordinary, nothing he could really get his ferret teeth into. Grattan? Others could fight over Grattan. And Mulholland. And the Landers, son and all.
"Tell me about Richard Ireland, will you? Is he playing it

the way his fans expect?" Kent kept pace as she was hustled away. "How's Mr. Cool, Miss Wilding?"

He was elbowed aside. Someone big and heavy complained: "Leave her alone, can't you? Fuck off."

He gained half a stride, leaning in. "Kent of the *Star*, Miss Wilding . . . Can I quote you as saying that Richard Ireland's playing a Nick Sudden role in there?"

"Are you mad?"

She was pretty hysterical, and he allowed for that. "How d'you mean, Miss Wilding?"

Then he saw the contempt in her eyes. He was getting her on a rebound and he caught the look head on, a glimpse of absolute truth. And he knew at once that no matter what else she might say—then or later—he'd got himself a real gold mine.

1:52 P.M.

WHEN Grattan put the bolt back on the door it was clear to Mulholland that the rage had almost spent itself. He stayed where he was, even so, not yet risking a move. The carpet was strewn with slivers of glass and smashed pottery and torn pieces of fabric, the dust of violence hanging on the ammoniac air. Only the softness around the edges of the curtains brightened the gloom.

A long time seemed to pass.

Grattan leaned against a cupboard, panting, the rifle back at the hip. "Come out of there." He faced the bathroom. "Out!"

Ireland didn't need any more. He opened up at once and stepped through to join them, hesitant as a blind man, broken, finished, the sudden block of light from the doorway making a silhouette of him.

"Over there."

Mulholland hadn't shifted an inch. He watched Grattan's

familiar peering as Ireland emerged, the rolling whiteness of his eyes as he struggled to master himself.

"Bitch," Grattan swore. "Filthy bitch."

He righted the chair he'd been using and sat down, cradling the gun.

"Because of her we do without." Childlike pique, yet savage, daunting. "No food. It stays where it is." He wiped his face, dark hair sweat-plastered down. "And from now on you take the phone." He looked at Ireland. "You, yes."

Mulholland said quickly: "Why not me?"

"Like hell."

"Why not do it yourself?" He chose his words. "The mystery's over. They know who you are."

Grattan glared, heavy-lidded, momentarily uncertain of himself. "You," he said to Ireland once again, apparently oblivious of what he'd done to him. Then his mind jerked somewhere else. "What's your height?"

"Five eleven."

"Weight?" Crazy questions.

"One hundred and seventy."

"And you?" Mulholland now.

"Five nine," Mulholland said, chancing something of his own. "What's this about?"

"Things we're going to do together."

"Like what?"

"Leaving here, for one."

Mulholland shifted a little. The worst dangers were yet to come. At least they weren't immediate, not while Grattan needed them and the frenzy had gone out of him. Enormous self-control was required as Mulholland sought to convey a sense of calm.

"Where do we go?"

No answer.

"When do we go?"

"D'you suppose I'd try it in daylight?" Grattan tossed his head, ridicule in the voice. "We go after dark, like I said."

Mulholland didn't press him. Six, seven hours to dark. He lit a cigarette and waited, hoping a show of indifference might provoke Grattan to divulge more. And eventually the waiting paid.

"Why d'you think I picked on you, Mulholland?"

"I guess the reason's pretty clear."

"What d'you reckon you're worth?"

Mulholland frowned.

"What's your safety worth?"

"How should I know that?"

"I'm asking two hundred thousand."

Mulholland took a few seconds. It had come to this, then. "Dollars?"

"Pounds," Grattan said. His mouth dragged. "Two hundred thousand pounds."

Another silence, smoke writhing away from the cigarette. "You'll never get it."

"Either I do or they don't get you." Malice warped Grattan's expression. "That's fair, isn't it? Reasonable? Either way it'll even up the score."

2:04 P.M.

THE TELEPRINTER started clattering, and Llewellyn glanced at the jerked-out text. *Neil James Grattan, 33, born Horsham, Sussex, no recorded next of kin. . . .*

To start with, Helen Olivares wasn't sure who was speaking. It didn't sound like Ireland, not as she thought he ought to sound.

"Two hundred thousand pounds," he told her weakly, echoing word for word, dry in the mouth and making a hash of the diction. "Two hundred thousand in used notes . . . Large denominations, nothing small. Packed in a valise . . ."

He began to stutter, losing it, and Grattan snatched the telephone out of his hand.

"Two hundred thousand," he grated. "I want it guaranteed within the hour. Then you'll hear what else. . . . And where, and how."

Lander was back in Ryder's office for the third time that day when the call came through. Ryder excused himself and took it. "Yes?" Then he said: "It's for you, Harry. . . . D'you want to have it here?"

"Sure."

Lander moved round the desk. "Hallo, this is Harry Lander. . . . That's correct, yes." He listened for a while, his face clouding. "Is that a fact? . . . At least twice, you say? And they're still around?" He twisted the cord indignantly in his fingers. "I most certainly will, yes. Right away. You bet. I'll be over right away to take him home. . . . Thank you."

"What's the trouble?" Ryder asked after a moment.

"Noel's school. Goddam reporters have been on his tail a couple of times this afternoon. Inside the school buildings, apparently. How d'you *like* that?" Incensed, Lander started for the door. "Isn't this what I've been talking about? The very thing? . . . Jesus Christ, it oughtn't to be allowed."

He slammed out, and Ryder shook his head. Behind his back the afternoon sky was heaped with blue-black clouds.

2:27 P.M.

McConnell and Dannahay went into the caravan together, crowding Llewellyn's work area.

"He's an amateur," McConnell said, "let's face it. And he's on his own."

"That's good?"

"Could have been all manner of ways worse. Could have been Black September, for instance. Could have been six people instead of one . . . anything. At least he's operating solo, and once he steps into the open his problems will multiply."

"He'll sure have it all to do," Dannahay added. "You're not haggling 'bout the money?"

"No."

"Certainly wouldn't advise it. Whatever he wants in that direction, the obvious thing's to play along. The amount's academic."

"Agreed." McConnell felt in a pocket for another peppermint. "How soon can your people let me have their report on Grattan?"

"Ten minutes? But the basic story you've been given's correct. Because of this wound of his, a bit of his brain doesn't function properly."

Llewellyn put in: "Beats me how he got the job in the first place."

"Securitywise he was okay. British soldier, honorable discharge—you know? Real satisfactory material on paper. I guess someone slipped up in the medical area and didn't indicate the *effect* of the physical damage done to him. Reckon that's what we'll find, that kind of thing. In any case, he obviously got the job through false pretenses, not being quite what he said he was." Dannahay blew a jet of smoke which flattened off the desk and spread. "We have congressmen like that. Presidents even, sometimes."

Mary Kay saw the first thin splashes of rain on the window as she spoke to her daughter in Philadelphia.

"Listen, Lois darling, and I'll tell you how it is. I don't know what you're getting on radio or whether there's television coverage yet, but Shelley's Hotel is only a stone's throw away

155

from the Embassy—you may remember it—and your father is in a room on the fifth floor about twenty rooms along from where I'm talking to you. . . . Yes; that's right. . . . He went in at ten o'clock London time in response to a demand from the gunman, and since then we've discovered this is a quite different person from the one everybody at first thought. . . . It's someone called Grattan, Lois, Grattan, and he used to be your father's driver here until a month or so ago. . . ."

For hours Mary Kay had somehow battened her emotions down, but Renata Lander had withdrawn from the room when Philadelphia was announced, and tears were on her cheeks now.

"One moment, Lois . . ."

She covered the mouthpiece in distress and hurriedly smeared the tears away, at all costs not wanting her voice to betray the extent of the anxiety ravaging her.

"There's been a demand for money within the last half hour —a huge sum. . . . Are you hearing me, Lois? . . . The probability is that negotiations about what finally's to happen won't come to a head until dark. Until then it's going to be a test of everyone's nerves, darling. . . . I know, oh I know. . . . So do something for your father, will you? I promised him I'd stay as close as possible all the time, and that I'm going to do. But would you go down to the church on the corner from where you are and pray for him? Would you, Lois? Join your prayers to mine? Pray that he'll have the strength he surely needs, and that everything's going to end right. . . ."

2:58 P.M.
"TELL HIM," McConnell instructed Helen Olivares, "he can have the money."

She relayed the message direct to Grattan; already he'd

done with using Ireland. He said nothing, nothing at all, and hung up immediately, like a man who didn't believe his luck. In the room, though, it was different.

"I undervalued you, Mulholland. I should have asked for a quarter of a million."

"There's nothing to stop you."

"That's right."

"But the more you ask, the bigger the bulk, the bigger the weight, the bigger your problems."

"Think I don't know?" Grattan's fingers spidered across the trigger guard. He glared suddenly, hollow-eyed. "What you trying to do? What you got in mind?"

"I don't understand."

"Talking that way. Trying to tell me what's what." He got up and crossed to the window, drawn there by the rain's faint tapping. A man he couldn't remember seeing before was positioned almost opposite behind the rooftop parapet. "Sod you," he muttered. Got a flak jacket on; bulky. Through a slit at the curtain's edge Grattan peered at the clouds and frowned.

Mulholland watched him. "They've guaranteed the money." There was a limit beyond which he dared not go. "So now what?"

"You talk too bloody much, that's what. So stuff it. Once and for all, stuff it."

He was sweating again, Mulholland noticed. And blinking, moving his scalp, as if a pain raged inside his head.

"Phil?"

"Without a doubt."

"I just this minute had a buzz about this guy Kent, Phil."

"Oh?"

"Someone who knows him better'n me says that once he starts playing hard to get you need to watch out."

The fat, balding man in the small plush office overlooking Piccadilly Circus winced as though he'd tasted something sour. "Tell me," he said without enthusiasm.

"He's playing hard to get, Phil."

"After being all over you?"

"Exactly. Can't get near him."

"Perhaps the smell of what he was going to do's gone up his nose same as it went up mine."

"Doesn't sound like the Howard Kent who makes a living."

"What d'you suggest, then?"

"Dunno. But I'm not certain I like it."

"Gone cool on Ireland, you mean?"

"I'm not so sure. Maybe I should wish he's done that. The girl's out, see? The bird he was with . . . And I'm just wondering what extra-special something she might have brought out with her that he's latched on to."

"Now," Richard Ireland's agent said, sharp with irritation, "you're talking bloody riddles again."

The four-hour weather-forecast map in New Scotland Yard's Control Room was brought up to date and the basic details immediately relayed to McConnell's caravan.

"Latest Met Office report warns of rain spreading from west, wind variable, becoming southwest, light. Maximum temperature 15 degrees C. . . . Okay?"

"Thanks," the constable said, taking it down through the soft-soft patter on the caravan's roof. "You may like to know you're right on cue."

"Shelley's Hotel." Helen Olivares was beginning to think if she said it one more time she would scream. "Hallo, yes?"

"I wish to speak to the police."

She switched the call across to the sergeant on the monitoring extension, but continued to listen.

"G'd afternoon. Who's speaking, please?"

"I prefer not to give my name." A man, gruff and peevishly brisk. "I've been onto the television companies but without getting a satisfactory answer. I think you ought to know of that at the outset, because it shows how irresponsible—"

"Is this a complaint, sir?"

"It's more than a complaint. It's a protest, in the name of common sense and the safety of all concerned. At least twice this afternoon normal television programs have been interrupted to give visual coverage of the situation in and around Shelley's Hotel . . ."

"Yes, sir."

". . . and it seems to me ludicrous that the police should permit the showing of their dispositions and be quoted as to their general plans and intentions when the gunman can watch these items himself. I've had the pleasure of staying at Shelley's in my time, and—"

"Excuse me, sir, but there *is* no TV in the room concerned."

"Eh?"

"The TV set in that particular room was removed yesterday for repair."

"Oh . . . I see."

"In any case, sir, there is always close liaison between the police and the media about such matters." The sergeant was young and police-college trained. "Thank you all the same for your vigilance."

He rang off. Well-meaning old blimp . . . Idiot.

3:37 P.M.

GRATTAN shuffled some broken glass underfoot and lifted the receiver. The rifle butt was hooked into his right armpit, and all the time the safety catch was being worked with his thumb —on, off; on, off.

"Get me the man who guaranteed the money."

"As soon as possible."

"Make it quick."

McConnell was halfway between the caravan and Shelley's when he was given the message. He ran from there, less on his toes now, out of breath when he arrived, and took the call in the night porter's cubicle to the rear of reception, a poster beside his head imploring him to winter in Bermuda.

"McConnell."

"You the one?"

"Yes."

"Same as used the loudspeaker at me?"

"Yes."

"I want more than the money."

Now it was coming. "What?"

"I want a helicopter. . . . *And* a plane. The helicopter here —in the square. The plane at Heathrow."

McConnell didn't hesitate. "When?"

"The helicopter's to be in the square no later than seven. On the ground and waiting."

"I don't know if a helicopter can land in the square."

"It can and it will."

"I'm agreeing to nothing that can't be done, d'you hear?" McConnell was feeling his way. "If a thing's possible—all right; there'll be no backing down. But I'm not—"

"There's space enough. If there isn't, make it. Get rid of some trees."

"I need half an hour before I'm able to answer that."

"There's only one answer."

McConnell could picture him—from the Embassy's photograph and from Gabrielle Wilding's description; then and now. He said defensively: "What would you settle for if a landing isn't possible in the time? . . . A car?" All along he'd imagined the demand would be for a car. "Would you settle for that?"

"No."

"We could arrange for a helicopter to use Hyde Park and have a car ferry you across." Anything, anything to get him outside.

"You're wasting time. It's got to be a helicopter, and it's got to be the square. By seven. I want evidence before I make a move. All I've had so far are promises."

McConnell sucked in a long, slow breath. "All right, all right. Say I can agree to . . ."

"You haven't any choice."

"When do you release those with you?"

"When I choose."

"Do it now and you'll come to no harm."

A snort. "I heard you before—over and over."

"Give me your word they'll be released."

"Everything depends on you. Double-cross me, shortchange me, and I won't be responsible. I want a four-, five-seater helicopter down in the square by seven o'clock, no later. I want a valise in it with the two hundred thousand. And I want an aircraft with a two-thousand-mile range fueled and ready for take-off at Heathrow."

"When by?"

"Ten. From ten on . . . I told you before, I don't make a move until dark." Grattan coughed. "And listen."

"Yes?"

"I've got things up my sleeve still. Other things."

"Like what?"

The line went dead immediately.

3:50 P.M.

DANNAHAY whistled. "Tell you what I figure?"

"Uh-huh."

"He's seen too many movies." He didn't smile.

"As long as I can draw him out of Shelley's," McConnell said, "I don't care what he's seen; or what he wants, or how or when."

"Does the square have space enough?"

"In front of the Roosevelt Memorial—no problem. I'll pull a Bell Jet Ranger over from Redhill. That ought to satisfy him."

There was silence, thoughts going in and around. Presently Dannahay said: "What about the Heathrow end?"

"It's not my intention to let him get that far. We'll have to settle it somehow between the hotel and the middle of the square."

"I've an idea or two about that. Suggestions—you know?"

"Good."

"The rain won't help."

"If it lasts," McConnell said thoughtfully, so long on the high wire now that he ached from the strain.

No more dead men. One, if it had to be, only if it had to be. But no more, please God, no more . . . That's how his thoughts went.

4:03 P.M.

LANDER left Noel at the house in Bruton Mews after he'd collected him from school.

"Now look," he explained. "It's essential I get back to the Embassy for a while." He didn't like leaving him alone, today especially. "While I'm gone, stay put—huh? No going out. No answering the door, or the phone even. If you do, ten to one

162

it'll be the press again—and you've had more than enough of that, you and your mother."

"Okay, Dad."

"Got any work to do? . . . Schoolwork?"

"Some."

"Okay." Lander nodded, making for the stairs. "I'll see you, then."

"Sure, Dad." All of a sudden Noel was into the game they played, their game, doing his James Stewart voice, eyes shining, deep in the timeless mysteries of fathers and sons. "Never want anything as bad to come our way again. It was hell, mister. . . ."

Kids were so damn resilient. "Bye," Lander said, disturbed, unable to rise to it.

A full hour ago, this was. Now Noel sat at the desk beneath the earth poster in his bedroom and wrote at length to his friend Jimmy Baatz in Columbus, Ohio.

You'll never guess what's happened here today, not in a hundred years of racking your brains. How would you like it if the police came to your house and told you and your mother that your old man had gone berserk with a rifle and holed himself up in a hotel room with the American Ambassador and a couple more hostages he'd gotten hold of? Well, that's exactly what happened to us here in London today, a real nightmare, somehow unbelievable even when it was still going on. For about three hours everyone was telling us my father was the one with the gun. Can you imagine it? The three hours seemed like years, believe me. And even though we knew, just knew, both of us, that he couldn't do anything bad like that, everything was pointing the other way. . . .

4:42 P.M.

AT THE DOOR of the Press Office at the Embassy Jake Shaw-cross said urgently to Dannahay: "I'm being pestered, John. What's this about parachutes?"

"He's asked for parachutes."

"Since when?"

"Minutes ago."

"Parachutes in the plural?"

"Unless McConnell's a liar."

"How many?"

"Six."

"*Six?*"

"That's the way it hit me too," Dannahay said.

"Why six, for God's sake?"

"Insurance?"

"Don't get you."

"For what it's worth, I'd say Grattan's aware how easy it is to arrange a chute malfunction." He picked a shred of tobacco from his lower lip. "All you gotta do is jam the rip-cord pins in their cones."

"He'd know about that?"

"Don't see why not."

"I thought he was a crazy guy."

"He was also a soldier, and soldiers learn all kinds of stuff."

"About free-fall jumping?"

Dannahay shrugged. "He can't order the plane to put down and then climb out of it and walk away. Hardly. So he jumps —there's nothing else. It's not original, but that's what he's planning to do. He picks his spot and jumps—anywhere within a coupla thousand miles of Heathrow."

"Mulholland too? Mulholland and the other—"

"Who can say? But one thing's a cinch. This is how he guarantees himself six good chutes. Who'd dare rig even one of them the way things are?"

164

"Yeah," Shawcross muttered. "Yeah."

"Gotta go now," Dannahay said, moving as he spoke. "McConnell quoted Grattan as saying he still has things up his sleeve, and it could well be. So we'll just have to sweat it out a few hours more. Wait an' see, in fact . . . *Ciao.*"

4:56 P.M.

GRATTAN herded the others into the bathroom with him, no relaxation of vigilance as he unzipped himself and used the toilet.

Ireland was nearest to the door. "I couldn't jump," he said.

It was all of twenty minutes since they'd heard Grattan's latest demand, and to Mulholland it had long since seemed that Ireland lacked any ability to respond.

"I couldn't do it."

He spoke as if Grattan wasn't there. Mulholland glanced at him sharply and saw how he rolled his head against the tiled wall, eyes closed tight, as if he were falling already. He must have been living with it.

"Couldn't . . . Couldn't."

"That's enough," Grattan snapped. "Button up."

Ireland opened his eyes and fixed them on Mulholland, moments passing as the terror continued to spiral, its delayed impact breaking out of him at last.

"Oh Christ," he said, the voice cracked now. "Not me."

Then he did an incredible thing. Like a sleepwalker, he turned from the wall and went through the door. Instinctively Mulholland pursued him, seven or eight steps across the chaos of the bedroom, Ireland accelerating, running.

"Don't be a fool!"

Appalled, Mulholland flung himself forward, dreading a bullet from behind. His arms pincered around Ireland's thighs and his right shoulder followed in as the tackle went home.

165

Ireland buckled and together they crashed to the floor, Mulholland uppermost, and even then his skin was crawling, despite the fact that Ireland didn't struggle.

"Get up"—Grattan.

Mulholland levered himself heavily to his feet, jarred by the impact.

"You as well ... *Move!*"

Ireland struggled into a sitting position, one cheekbone grazed.

"Another try like that and it'll be your last."

Mulholland heard himself say: "Let him go."

Grattan stood in the bathroom doorway, pulling up his fly.

"What use is he to you?" Mulholland said wearily. "You know darned well—"

"Don't tell me what I know."

"All I'm trying to point out—"

"*Don't!*" Grattan barked. "I'm up to here with being told. Told, always told. Where to go, what to do—always fucking told." His eyes blazed, hatred in them, his raised arm a muscle-twitch away from swiping Mulholland across the face. "That's over, Mulholland. All that piss and wind of yours is dead and gone."

Mulholland turned his back on him and spoke exclusively to Ireland. "He needs us when he chooses to walk out of here —right? Across the square he'll need us, between the square and the airport he'll need us, in the plane he'll still need us. But not after that."

He was talking to a man whose nerve had completely gone, holding him by the shoulders, spelling out what he himself had concluded almost as soon as Grattan had slammed the receiver down on McConnell.

"No one's going to jump out of any plane," he continued evenly, "except him." He shook Ireland gently and attempted a feeble grin. "D'you suppose he wants us around forever?"

It cost him something to dredge such calm. His heart was thudding, and his lips kept sticking to his teeth; but he wasn't finished yet. Once more he appealed to Grattan, Grattan who'd exchanged uniforms, soldier to chauffeur, and then been found wanting, Grattan whom he pitied as well as feared.

"I'm the one, Grattan. Just me. You don't need him at all."

"Wrong."

"When we go out of here, you can keep me as close as a Siamese twin." He had no illusions; there would be no immunity. "You can handle me, sure. Me alone. You'll never be able to cope with the pair of us."

They eyed one another. "Are we there, sir? . . . Is this the place, sir?"—vividly Mulholland could remember him, lost and alarmed and useless, trying to cover again and again. But the tone was very different now, the thinking suddenly rational.

"You've got it all wrong, Mulholland. I'd be a sight better off with more, not less. I'd rather have three of you, at least three."

5:16 P.M.

THE THIN-FACED croupier with the ringed fingers and bored, unblinking stare had two numbers he could call. No one answered the first; on the second he got Knollenberg.

"Will you want me to keep a check tonight? . . . If he shows?"

"No."

"Just the once more, I was told."

"Probably that."

"But not tonight?"

"Not tonight," Knollenberg said. "Call one of us back tomorrow, will you? We're sort of tied up with something else right now."

"YES, SIR," McConnell said to the Commissioner. "I've had confirmation that Redhill is releasing a helicopter at 1825 with a Grosvenor Square ETA of 1850. Airport Police are meanwhile in contact with British Airways about the provision of a suitable medium-range aircraft at Heathrow. If it's impossible for any reason, they'll go to one of the charter companies—though I don't anticipate any difficulty in that direction. . . . The civil pilot will need to be a volunteer, of course. . . . Yes, yes, that's understood."

Tense and red-eyed, he gazed through the caravan window at the rain; it was lightish still but steady.

"The Prime Minister? . . . Well, no one's more anxious than we are, sir. Or more determined . . ."

There were enough pressures without that. Anyone would think there were grades of effort.

Roberto Olivares woke from a five-hour sleep with guilt on his mind and reached for the telephone, his tongue probing the soft crater in his gum.

"Helen?"

"What is it?" Tired and offhand. "You all right?"

"I've been asleep, Helen."

"Lucky you."

"I was bleeding something awful. . . . Hell, I could have died, the way it was."

"Oh, come on."

"You've no idea."

She let it go. "You able to do something now?"

"Right away." Of *course*, the tone implied. Then: "What's happening? What's the situation?" Before she could answer he went on: "I'm sorry, Helen." Little-boy contrite. "Real sorry."

She let that go as well. "The basic situation hasn't changed.

But things are building to a head, so the sooner you can make a contribution—"

"Sure."

"We'll probably have to evacuate."

"Evacuate Shelley's? . . . God in heaven!"

"If you'd been around a bit more today, you wouldn't sound so stupidly theatrical." For once her anger flared. "Or be so ignorant."

"You and your stars," he flung back. "How about *them?* They didn't know bloody anything either."

"Come on down," she said. Incredibly she could smile, and with affection. "Grow up, and come on down to help."

5:56 P.M.

THE LIGHT coming from the bathroom showed the instability etched into Grattan's face.

"McConnell?"

"McConnell, yes."

"What about the helicopter?"

"It'll be in the square by seven. . . . Before seven."

"With the money?"

"With the money. And the plane at Heathrow—"

"The plane can wait. First things first. What time d'you make it?"

"Almost six."

"There're some other things I want."

"Tell me."

"I don't want 'em now. Not until the helicopter's down."

"Right." A frenzy of scratching raced along the wire. "Tell me," McConnell said grimly.

"Four pistols. One real, with ammunition. The other three imitation."

McConnell frowned. *Four?*

"Get that?"

"Yes." He thought of the tray of coffee and sandwiches still lying uncollected in the corridor. "Where do you want them?"

"Here."

"Outside the door?" Like a servant.

"Inside the room."

McConnell frowned again, in dread all the time of the single miscalculation that could bring disaster landsliding down. *"Inside?"*

"The girl's the last one to be allowed out of here until we all come out together."

"You want delivery made to the door, is that it? Right to the door?"

"Not to the door. How many more times? . . . Listen. Listen and get it straight."

McConnell nodded, alone. Grattan had an audience.

"Four pistols. Three of them fakes . . . models, imitations. The other one a real one, police issue, with plenty of ammunition."

"Right."

"Delivered in a box. Or a bag, paper bag."

"Right."

"And the man who delivers is to enter the room."

"Right."

"There's also a special requirement about the man."

"Such as?"

"Weight and height. I want him between one seventy and one eighty pounds, between five ten and six feet."

"Why, for God's sake?"

"Because he stays, that's why."

"Now, look—"

"Whoever comes in stays in—until I'm ready. Until dark."

"It's no good, Grattan. I'm not giving you anyone else."

"You are, you know."

McConnell could hear him breathing.

"You are," Grattan told him, hard as iron. "Otherwise I shoot the actor."

He let it hang, waiting.

"I can manage with Mulholland if I have to, him and him alone. But with three I can manage better. . . . So make up your mind."

DUSK

DANNAHAY drew the money out of special funds, as arranged. Only the amount was abnormal as far as he was concerned, and he looked it over before snapping down the locks: the two hundred thousand pounds fitted the valise as compactly as if it were custom-built.

"Keep a guard on that," he told Osborne, "like it all belongs to you and me."

"Where d'you want it held?"

"Right here." Osborne's ground-floor office at the Embassy. "And on call at a moment's notice—whenever McConnell says."

"How's McConnell going to take Grattan?"

"There's only one way, I guess, but he sort of wants to avoid using his sharpshooters if he can. Last I was with him he was planning on making a final appeal to the guy to quit."

"D'you see that happening?"

"No," Dannahay said. "Not a chance. McConnell'll try, though—and I'd be doing exactly the same in his shoes. But Grattan's hardly going to change his mind at this stage. If anything, I'd say he'll step up his demands—remember that Dallas affair, month or two back? Asking for the moon at the end. It happens, you know. The power thing gets them, I s'ppose."

"What I recall of Grattan he was pretty mild-mannered. Strange, isn't it? Slow, too. Not exactly a ball of fire."

"He's got a gun now," Dannahay said. "That's what makes the difference. McConnell isn't going to find it easy, no matter how he sets the scene—not with the rain and the dark and all."

6:11 P.M.

"WHEN THIS is all over," Mary Kay Mulholland said with a small dry laugh that was all nerves, "I'm never going to keep another clock in the house. Never . . . Or wear a watch, even."

Renata Lander understood. This was how it had been while her own nightmare had lasted—the minute hands scarcely moving, the hour hands seemingly stuck fast. An entire afternoon had passed since she'd come to join Mary Kay, and she'd seen it slowly take its toll. Others had come and gone, some more than once—the Foreign Secretary with a personal message from the Queen, Sam and Margaret O'Hare, Robbie Ryder, secretaries from the Embassy, staff from Winfield House, McConnell several times; but no one could more than touch the surface of Mary Kay's loneliness, no one completely share the spun-out stress and uncertainty. These were hers and hers alone.

Renata Lander looked out at the rain and downward into North Audley Street and right into Grosvenor Square. From this end of the hotel almost half of the square was visible, nothing moving there, nobody, the silence as implacable now as throughout the day, the paved walks across the grass glistening in the wet and the light poor, like a premature dusk.

"More coffee?"—for the nth time.

173

"No."

"Cigarette?"

"No." Mary Kay shook her head. "No, thanks." A minute later she was smoking again.

"It's getting gloomy out there." Renata Lander left the window, stillness in the streets, stillness in the corridor, no escape from what it meant, nothing to relieve the gnawing tension.

"Three hours, and it'll be dark. Only three hours more and—"

"Don't talk about time," Mary Kay broke in, courage still intact but her years showing. "Time's a cheat and a fraud."

6:15 P.M.

GRATTAN peered through the gap where the curtains joined, only a narrow portion of the square to be seen from 501, no view at all of where the helicopter would put down, the Navy Building in the way.

Since he'd finished with McConnell he'd become increasingly agitated, muttering, unsettled, back and forth across the room.

"McConnell?" He'd snatched up the phone again.

"Not here," Helen Olivares said. "But I—"

"Give him a message."

"Yes."

"Tell him there's more to be brought in. Other things. Over and above the pistols."

"What are they?"

"Overcoats. Long dark overcoats . . . Four of each."

She repeated it, scribbling.

"And wigs. Four identical wigs."

"Four wigs?" Her surprise showed.

"Wigs for men."

"I'll pass the message."

Grattan hung up, both hands on the gun again. He seemed lost inside himself for a moment or two; then he singled out Mulholland, a look of anticipated triumph in the wildness of his stare.

"When we go out of here," he said, "none of those sods will know who's who."

6:19 P.M.
McCONNELL was leaving the caravan when Dannahay intercepted him.

"See you've had a touch-down point marked out for the chopper."

"Uh-huh."

"More space over there'n you'd figure. Won't even spoil the rose beds."

They walked side by side, their raincoat collars up. The rain was soft and vertical, no breeze. They crossed Upper Brook Street, the Roosevelt Memorial showing dark through the trees beyond the place where Eddie Raven had died.

Dannahay said: "I picked out three or four good spots for your SPG men. Can you spare a coupla minutes?"

"There's something you should know first."

"Yeah?"

"He wants another person sent in."

"*Another* one?"

McConnell nodded. "That's not all. He's being choosy about the person's build."

"What the hell for?"

"Safety in numbers? Weight, height—he's looking for an approximation to Ireland and himself. That's my guess. Five ten to six feet, one seventy to one eighty pounds."

"Smart, this Grattan."

"No other reason for it that I can see."

"Smarter'n I gave him credit for," Dannahay mused. "So what're you going to do?"

"I've no choice. Someone goes in."

"Who you going to send?"

"One of my fellows."

"When?"

"After the helicopter's down. In about an hour, say. Grattan hasn't said before."

He told Dannahay about the pistols, real and imitation, and Dannahay whistled like a cooing bird. "He sure has you by the short and hairy ones."

"Not forever . . . Not for long."

Dannahay shot him a glance of appraisal. Deceptive guy, McConnell. Not all on the surface.

"Shall I show you where I'd position the SPG?"

"Please."

They made their way into Grosvenor Square, the Navy Building covering their movements once they had crossed North Audley Street. The square was like an arena, walled in on all sides, red brick and white stone beyond the trees. Dannahay argued the reasons for the placings he suggested—a maximum of opportunity with a minimum risk of crossfire danger—one marksman to the side of the Roosevelt plinth, two others at right angles from there, the first by an elm, the second under a dripping chestnut.

"Only suggestions, mind," Dannahay said.

"Thanks."

"If it comes to that."

"Thanks."

Normality lay beyond the barriers. The muted groan of traffic reached them from Park Lane and Oxford Street and Berkeley Square, commuters going home, London changing hands. They started back, treading through the puddles.

"He'll never accept one of your guys as the extra man," Dannahay said presently.

"He won't be told."

"Sometimes it kind of shows. People like Grattan have their antennas out. They smell the air—you know? Last thing I want to do's put a shot across your bows, David, but any move that could add to the danger Mulholland's in has got to be a bad one."

"And this adds to it?"

"It could. I'd say that Grattan hates your people. And if he so much as sniffs one's in there with him . . ." Dannahay spread his hands, eyes sharp as a fox's. "See what I mean?"

"Of course."

"I'm not f'r a minute making out—"

"Who d'you suggest goes in, then?"

"Mind if I come back on that?"

"It'll have to be soon."

They parted at the foot of the Embassy steps, Dannahay mounting them two at a time, McConnell hurrying toward the caravan. All day, it suddenly struck him, he hadn't been in touch with his wife.

In the caravan there were too many things at once—telephones, people thudding in and out, voices, questions, doubts . . . always doubts.

"Wigs, eh?" McConnell had an extraordinary feeling that Grattan was somehow tightening his grip. "Wigs and overcoats . . . Where the hell, at this time of evening—"

Llewellyn said: "The wigs you'll get from Maison Georges, Buckingham Palace Road." Knew everything, Llewellyn.

"This late?"

"They'll bend over backward. What's more, they're the best in the business. The very best."

"Overcoats?"

"Overcoats are easy," Llewellyn said, then shouted: "Sergeant!"

Simultaneously, someone else was adding to the babble. "Redhill helicopter airborne and on its way . . ."

6:30 P.M.

"HERE IS the LBC news coming to you on 417 meters on the medium wave band. . . . First, the Grosvenor Square siege, where the situation remains outwardly unchanged. The gunman has demanded a helicopter to lift him and his two hostages to Heathrow and a plane to be on stand-by at the airport. There are unconfirmed reports that he is now asking for a third man to join Ambassador Ralph Mulholland and the actor Richard Ireland in Room 501 at Shelley's Hotel. The police neither confirm nor deny this story, though Detective Chief Superintendent David McConnell, who is directing operations, continues to stress that whenever necessary he will accede to the gunman's demands if opposition to them might in any way increase the threat to the hostages' lives. . . ."

6:32 P.M.

"GOT A MOMENT?" Dannahay asked, head poked into Lander's office on the Defense Attaché's floor.

"Sure."

"Been a bad day for you, huh? A real twenty-two-carat shit of a day."

"Wouldn't want another like it, I can tell you. Not ever."

"I bet."

Dannahay sauntered in, and Lander left his desk, long-legged and restless.

"Could you use a Scotch?"

"Just about." Dannahay nodded. "But small, real small."

"No ice, I'm sorry."

"I'll survive."

His gaze scattered about him while Lander opened up a file cabinet. From the window he could clearly see the broad north-south walk in front of the Roosevelt Memorial and the white daub where the helicopter was to put down beyond the candled chestnut tree.

Lander said: "It's hard to believe—all of it. Not just what happened to me. That Mulholland's actually on the rack, for instance, right now, and only a couple of hundred yards away. Despite all the evidence"—he nodded into the waiting square—"and knowing what happened to Noel and Renata, and Renata being over there with Mary Kay, and the radio and TV peep shows and the police and every damn thing . . . Despite all of that it still seems kind of unreal."

"How well did you know Grattan?"

Lander shrugged. "I rode with him a couple of times. And like everyone else I saw him around."

"How'd he pick it up, d'you reckon, that you belonged to a rifle club?"

"I told him." Lander drank. "Sometimes when you're traveling together a thing like that slips out. And he was interested, what with his background. . . . Come to think of it, he knew I kept the gun at the house—and where. He saw where. I remember now. Dropped me home one time when I had the case with me, and he came inside to use the phone. That's why the bastard—"

"You hit it off with him? That's what I'm getting at."

"He seemed all right. Lousy driver, erratic as could be." Lander paused, one eyebrow slowly rising. "Say, where's this taking me?"

Dannahay licked his lips. "Got a favor to ask."

"Yes?"

"Very special."

"Yes?"

"You won't like it."

"For Christ's sake," Lander protested.

Dannahay's eyes hadn't left him. "Grattan wants another man to go in."

"I heard about . . ." Lander broke off, stock still. "Hey, *wait* a minute. . . ." Incredulity shaped the line of his mouth. "You aren't . . . you aren't seriously suggesting it might be me?"

"I am." No bones about it. "Yeah."

"You think I'm expendable or something?" Lander laughed sharply. "How long've you nursed this great idea?"

"Five minutes."

"*Me?*"

"I was walking down there"—Dannahay pointed—"with McConnell, and he was telling how he was going to use one of his own guys."

"And . . ." Very terse.

"I reckon it ought to be one of ours. . . . It's as simple as that."

"Me?" Lander repeated, still incredulous.

"You can always say no."

"I'd be a fool if I said anything else."

"On the other hand I'd argue you've a sort of obligation to say yes."

Indignation, concern, disbelief—they all showed. "After what's happened already?"

"Because of what's happened already."

"You'd better explain that. From where I stand—"

"I'm talking 'bout Mulholland," Dannahay said.

"On the contrary"—Lander shook his head, touchy as hell—"you're talking about me. And you're expecting me to buy some spur-of-the-moment idea by wrapping it up with mention of obligations."

180

"If that's how you see it, Harry."

"How else should I see it, for God's sake?"

Dannahay's eyes were bead-bright. "Mulholland thought he was going into that room because of you."

"He'd have gone in anyway."

"You can't prove it."

"Aw, come on," Lander flared. "Don't try and lay everything at my door. I've been used enough today."

"I'm not using anybody," Dannahay said evenly. "I'm just putting a certain proposition forward . . . and giving reasons why."

"No," McConnell said. "I have no statement. No . . . Later, possibly, but not now. No statement now."

"I got other reasons," Dannahay told Lander. "Not just the way you might feel about Mulholland."

"Such as?"

"Scares me, really scares me, how Grattan might operate if he finds the fuzz in the room with him. I'm all for him being acquainted with the extra man. Last thing in the world we want is for him to get jumpy and suspicious—more'n he'll be in any case—just when he's planning to move out."

Lander said nothing. Already his glass was empty.

"McConnell's going to have one more try at making him quit, but it'll never work. Grattan won't come out until his demands are met, and, among other things, that means someone going in. Preferably, like I say, someone he knows. Not just anyone either. Someone your height, Harry. Your build."

Dannahay sipped his whisky.

"They're the same as his, Harry—give or take a little. Same as the actor's . . . You see? Between Shelley's and where the chopper'll be, Grattan's aiming to confuse."

"I don't understand."

"Come over here." Against his will Lander followed Dannahay to the window. "How far," Dannahay said, "between the two—hotel and there? Three hundred yards?"

"Perhaps."

"He'll be more vulnerable once he's walking than at any other time—and he knows it. So he's taking what precautions he can."

"Gabrielle Wilding's asleep, I'm afraid," a girl answered. "She's had a terrible experience today, as you may know, and the doctor's given her heavy sedation. Who shall I tell her called? Her mother? It's such a bad line. . . . Her mother, did you say?"

"Listen," Dannahay said. "There's another good reason I thought of you."

"Tell me."

"Those voices you do . . . those impersonations."

Lander puckered his forehead. "You're going too fast again."

"McConnell has to rely on a marksman picking Grattan off somewhere inside those three hundred yards. Oh yeah—that's what it'll come to, no mistake. And I can see him having problems, seconds ticking away and his chances going with them. It'll be dark, remember. No moon, no stars, too many people looking alike."

"So?"

"I favor a distraction. Grattan's flaw is his visual memory—right? But throw an unexpected voice at him when he's halfway across the square and I figure his reaction will single him out like someone put a flashlight full on his face."

Dannahay tilted his head.

"There's no one else I know could do this, Harry. Only you. You qualify all round."

Lander's glance was almost bitter. "You sure lay it on, don't you?"

"Harry, I reckon it's a duty, the way things are."

Crouched behind the roof parapet of the building facing Shelley's, a rain-sodden policeman thought he saw the curtain twitch in 501. He gave a warning whistle to his nearest colleague and crouched lower, rifle at the ready. Nothing else happened, but he reached for his radio and reported in.

Bloody stalemate, this was.

Lander was staring at the moss-colored carpet, his mind on the main chance. Grattan had focused a spotlight on him, dangerous assumptions had readily been made—assumptions that, despite everything, could stick and jeopardize the future. No smoke without fire . . . What Dannahay suggested now could redress the damage done; there was merit to be earned, even honor.

"There . . . there's Renata to be considered. Renata and—"

"D'you suppose I don't know?"

"I need time," Lander said.

"Sure . . . sure." Watching him, Dannahay said: "I oughta warn you, though—there isn't much of that to play with." He drained his glass and put it carefully down on the desk. "Tell you something else, just one more thing—in case you figure this is all off the top of my head and you're being pressured without due thought."

"Yeah?"

"We can minimize the risks. I wouldn't go to McConnell with the idea if I didn't believe that. I wouldn't have spoken to you in the first place, even."

6:47 P.M.

GRATTAN heard the helicopter a fraction before either of the others. At first it was no louder than the fly that had buzzed against the glass, and he grunted, standing still in the darkened, sweat-sharp room, eyes wandering as he tried to place the direction of approach.

The Mulhollands were a corridor's length apart, but they heard it simultaneously, Renata Lander as well, and she hurried to the window, biting her lower lip as she vainly searched the sky.

Dannahay, Llewellyn, McConnell, Lander, Savage—all of them heard it within seconds of each other, the sound growing in volume and becoming dominant, turning their heads to the south and southwest.

From his car in Park Lane the Commissioner also heard the guttural throbbing, and he screwed his neck trying to glimpse how close it was. Pretty low, he reckoned, and plumb overhead as his driver cornered by the Grosvenor House Hotel.

Lander and Dannahay were the first to sight it. It came farting angrily across the upper right-hand corner of the Indonesian Embassy, dark blue, POLICE emblazoned in white on its side, the big blades flailing the grey rain. Lander put its height at about two hundred feet as the forward motion slowed and it began to hang above the center of the square, nose-heavy, waggling its tail from side to side as the pilot maneuvered.

On the ground a couple of policemen emerged from cover and took up position close to the touch-down mark, guiding the helicopter in like a flight-deck crew. Renata Lander and Mary Kay were able to watch it sink behind the screen of trees in a vapor of spray, but from 501 this was impossible; Grattan never saw it. For him there was only the snarling reverberation as it closed on the mark and then the silence

184

when the pilot cut the motors and the Bell Jet Ranger settled like a mosquito on the feed.

Yet this satisfied him. He laughed, that awful curt laugh, as if only now he really believed the extent of his power.

6:29 P.M.

THE COMMISSIONER of Police stroked his shiny bald scalp as he listened to McConnell explain about the additional hostage Grattan had demanded, and the weapons, real and false, and the four overcoats and the wigs. He was a large craggy man with a damaged left ear, a legacy from amateur boxing days, and he stood like a boxer, the stance still aggressive. Arming Grattan with a pistol wasn't something he could question, not with McConnell under extreme duress, but he didn't like it. Or the third man. On the table in front of him was the sketch Llewellyn had made, a circled H indicating the helicopter and three small crosses in roughly the positions Dannahay had suggested for the marksmen.

He said: "You'll have another go at him of course? One more appeal?"

"One more."

"And if you draw a blank?"

"If I draw a blank, sir," McConnell answered, "we'll have reached a point of no return."

The Commissioner didn't believe in meddling. But the buck would stop with him, and he wanted no buck, no disaster, no chance of being pilloried. So half-measures were out. Too much was at stake for high-wire indecision. McConnell knew what he was doing, none better, and he'd obviously got his priorities right.

"I agree," the Commissioner grated. "If it comes to that, you'll have no option but to put Grattan down." He sounded as if he were speaking about an animal. "Who's volunteered to go in?"

McConnell heaved his shoulders. "The Americans have offered to make a contribution in that direction."

"Oh?"

"Suits me. As long as whoever they choose doesn't ball everything up by trying to be clever."

6:29 P.M

LANDER refilled his glass and gulped the whisky down. The future would repay him. He gazed from the Embassy window at the helicopter squatting in front of the Roosevelt Memorial and felt the pressure of time and the weight of Dannahay's persuasiveness.

He had come a long way in the last half hour. Grattan was still to be distracted by the sudden use of a strange voice; that was agreed. But now the suggestion was that Lander should carry a gun himself rather than rely on the effectiveness of McConnell's marksmen. And the extraordinary thing was that he had contributed to the change of plan, more anxious to be armed out there than not, putting the notion forward and having Dannahay then come up with an idea as to how it might be done.

"I reckon," he said to Dannahay slowly, "it's my turn now to ask a favor."

"Such as?"

"Your selling it all to Renata the way you sold it to me."

"Sure," Dannahay said, with a glance that could have meant anything. "If you can't handle it, sure." He gripped Lander by the arm, allies, schemers together. "Grattan'll have a whole lot more going for him than McConnell seems to realize—and he hasn't necessarily played all of his cards yet. So this extra man has gotta be better'n a dummy—see, Harry? Someone

186

passive out there's exactly what this guy Grattan's after."

How strained Lander looked: pinched.

"You're the one who can tip this thing McConnell's way, I'm sure of it," Dannahay said. "But first I gotta talk with him —so keep your fingers crossed."

Airport Police confirm a BAC One Eleven will be on stand-by at Heathrow as from 2200 hours. . . .

Llewellyn glanced up from the message pad and peered through the caravan's misted-over window. "What time's sunset?"

"Twenty thirty-six," the sergeant at his elbow said. "Precisely."

"So it'll be dark—"

"Half an hour later? Nine-ten . . . nine-fifteen? Somewhere about then."

7:04 P.M.

SAVAGE'S EYES seemed to be bulging out of his head with fatigue and his mustache looked more than ever as if it were painted on.

"Give me the hailer, will you?" McConnell said grimly.

The Commissioner had traveled in the elevator with him. Along with Savage they stood together in the angle of wall by the stairs. Without appearing to, McConnell braced himself. No telephone this time, no danger of being cut off. Grattan was going to hear every word.

"Listen, Grattan. Listen to what I have to say. . . . It's in your best interests to listen."

Depending on what was said, and how it was said, the situation might change. *Might.* McConnell wasn't optimistic, but this was a chance that had to be taken.

"First, let me tell you what's been arranged—and is being

arranged—on your behalf. . . . The helicopter's down in the square—that much you'll know. Within the next fifteen minutes or so a valise packed with the two hundred thousand pounds will be put aboard. In addition, I have just received word that an aircraft is in readiness and awaiting further instructions at Heathrow. . . . Make a note of all this, Grattan. The overcoats and the wigs are being obtained, and we're seeing to it that you get the hand guns you asked for. . . ."

McConnell faced along the corridor. Behind his back Renata Lander and Mary Kay Mulholland had been drawn from their room by the cavernous vibration of his voice.

"I'm telling you this so you can see the lengths to which we're prepared to go to accommodate you. But you must also be made aware of the fact that you can't possibly succeed. No one gets away with this sort of thing. World over it's the same. The odds are too great. D'you hear me, Grattan? The odds are too great."

Last time there had been a shot through the door, warning him off. But not now. All there was now was the metallic boom of his own voice chasing along the walls and the self-same sense of futility, nothing going to come of it, words against a damaged mind and the power of a gun.

"You're an amateur, Grattan. How far d'you hope to get? There'll be parachutes in the plane at Heathrow—okay, that's a fact. But whichever way you choose to be flown, and wherever you decide to jump, your position will be plotted. . . . Don't you see that? You can't get away. You'll be trapped the same as you are now. It stands to reason."

McConnell paused, so tense that his hands were trembling.

"I'm asking one thing of you, Grattan. That's all. Just the one thing . . . Come on out of there. Leave the gun and come out into the corridor. There'll be no shooting. You have my personal guarantee that if you quit now your own safety will be respected. If no one is harmed, you will come to no harm yourself. . . ."

He glanced quickly at the Commissioner, who stood with pursed lips. Then he plunged again, the final time.

"I'm going to give you a minute, Grattan. I've made you an offer and I'm waiting for you here in the corridor. For God's sake, man, be sensible and do as I say. *Come on out.* . . . You've got a minute to act, a whole minute, starting now."

His eyes locked without much hope on the closed door. Including the SPG there were eight people in the corridor, and not one of them moved an inch, staring, wire-taut, an age passing as they waited. But they waited in vain. There was no response, no movement, the quiet itself as much an answer as a jeer of defiance.

McConnell glanced at the Commissioner again. The Commissioner caught the look and shook his head. Even so, McConnell delayed a little more, twenty seconds or so more, nearer two minutes than one going by before he acknowledged failure.

To Savage he then said: "I want your three best men, Bunny."

"How soon?"

"Within the hour." He'd never given such an order. "And I want each of 'em issued with the night-sight rifle."

7:08 P.M.

GOD KNOWS about Ireland, who'd as good as lost touch, but Mulholland experienced no despair when Grattan ignored McConnell's appeal. He'd expected nothing else. All along, so it had seemed to him, Grattan would go through with his plans, hell-bent in his madness on a course that was doomed from the outset. The girl must have told McConnell how it was in 501, *must* have, all manner of things she must have put him wise to; so he'd have a heap of information that wasn't his before she escaped—everything, apparently, except the certainty that Grattan couldn't be deflected from taking on the world.

Grattan leaned against the wall and stretched down for the telephone.

"Yes?" All day Helen Olivares hadn't once been found wanting.

"There's a message for McConnell."

"Yes?"

"When the other man comes in, he's to bring a flashlight."

"I'll pass the message."

"And something else. He's to be in here by half eight. No later."

"Half eight."

"Overcoats, wigs, pistols, and a flashlight—got that?"

"Yes," she said.

"On top of which two other things. Every light in this hotel and every street light for a quarter mile around is to be switched off." He repeated this more slowly, watching Ireland, watching Mulholland, eyes alert, aware, unblinking in the shadows of the room. "Every single one. *Off*, d'you hear?"

McConnell was handed the scribbled note the moment he emerged into the foyer from the elevator. It seemed to the Commissioner that he read it at least twice before passing it over.

"What—" the Commissioner began impatiently.

"He's playing chess with us, sir, that's what. One damn move after another."

DANNAHAY NODDED. "Gets smarter as he goes along—wouldn't you say?"

McConnell scowled, enough on his mind without that, uneasy now, tomorrow's headlines in the making.

"Don't want to get under your feet," Dannahay said, suddenly as tactful as could be, "but can you spare a minute?"

"Sure."

"About the guy who's to go in?"

"Sure."

"Remember I said I felt it ought to be one of our own people?"

"I do, yes."

"I can make out a case for it being Lander."

"*Lander?*"

"A good case." Dannahay was nothing if not direct. "And I'll tell you why."

"Lander?" McConnell repeated, still surprised. "Now hold on a moment. To begin with, what makes you think he'd agree? After what's happened to him and to his—"

"We've discussed it already."

"And he's said yes?"

"That's right. He thought it over."

"My God."

"I haven't fallen off the edge of my mind, you know. And I didn't stick a pin in the State Department directory, anything like that. I went for Lander. I simply figured you're going to need him."

"Why him? Why him especially?"

They were close to the big glass doors that opened onto North Audley Street, the street dead and empty in the rain. In two hours' time it would be as black as pitch out there.

McConnell tried once more. "How d'you mean—need him?"

Dannahay listed two of Lander's qualifications, ticking them off on stocky fingers. Lander's build, one. Lander being known to Grattan, two . . . Neither impressed McConnell, who said as much, time slipping by and making him edgy.

"Look, if you feel there's a special reason why it should be one of your people—fine. I've no objection, none. But I can't for the life of me see why you've singled out Lander. Poor bastard's had enough for one day, I'd have thought, and there must be plenty of others who qualify equally well."

"Wouldn't dispute that f'r a moment," Dannahay said. "But there's something Lander can do the others can't. He can do voices."

"And that's important?"

"Absolutely. The way some people can fool you with cards, so Lander can catch you out with voices . . . impersonations."

"I'm nowhere near you," McConnell said. There were moments when his brain seemed to stall from sheer fatigue. He fingered his jaw, rasping the stubble, and made another start. "Grattan's after an extra decoy. An out-and-out decoy."

"But one you can use, for God's sake." Dannahay began pocket-tapping for cigarettes. "I'll give it to you straight, David. I'm shit-scared something'll go wrong. Everything's running for Grattan, and he's sure been putting on the pressure—like this dousing all the lights, f'r instance. You know, once the four of them come out of here, the only one we'll be a hundred per cent sure of's Mulholland. He's thicker, shorter. *If* we can see him at all, mind."

"The night sights will still pick him up."

"Okay, okay. But what about the others? Complete darkness, good as, and this rain. They'll look more alike than carbon copies." He flipped a cigarette into his mouth and lit it, eyes slitted against the smoke. "If you're really expecting to get lucky out there in the square you'll need all the help you can think of . . . Lander's help."

McConnell had never known Dannahay more anxious, or

more pressing. He eyed him thoughtfully. A night-sight rifle had an almost total-darkness capacity; its image-intensifier could concentrate what natural light there was by up to 80.000 times. Inevitably, though, with conditions the way they were going to be, its effectiveness was sure to be reduced. He had no illusions about this. He knew the risks and he accepted the responsibility. But Dannahay had a point: Grattan's latest demand had tipped the initiative a shade in his own favor.

"Tell me what you've got in mind," McConnell said, thinking as he spoke, weighing possible pros and cons. "Spell it out for me." Dannahay's suggestions about the positioning of the marksmen were very sound; he acknowledged that. "Is the idea to confuse Grattan in some way? Is that what you're saying?"

"In part."

"Lander using a bogus voice?"

"He does 'em like they're real—you've no idea. It's his fun thing; he and his boy sort of compete sometimes." Dannahay inhaled like a man come up for air. "My opinion, the shock of a strange voice'll be enough to throw Grattan right off guard—just long enough for Lander to take him."

"How?"

"Hand gun," Dannahay said. "He's a great shot, too, which is another reason why. Real good with guns of all sorts."

"He'd never get away with it."

"He's willing to try—with sharpshooters in support."

"No, no . . . Grattan will search him the moment he enters the room. That's as sure as we're standing here."

"He doesn't take the gun *in* with him, David. He collects it on the way *out.*"

"Where from?"

"Here." Dannahay stepped toward the large bronze discus-shaped handles mounted on the entrance doors. "Tape a pistol to the reverse side. . . . Behind, see? . . . Light but

193

firm. Anyone knowing it's there can slide it off as he's passing. Nothing to it. Easier than getting wet."

McConnell took his time. "Lander knows about this?"

"I put it to him."

"And he agreed?"

"In principle, yeah. Like I say, he came around to seeing your problems."

McConnell seemed to be expecting him to say something more, so Dannahay went on.

"Main thing to sway him, I guess, is being aware Mulholland went upstairs under the wrong impression. You could say that kinda puts him under an obligation. On top of which he's got a real talent with this voice thing, as well as with a gun. He knows the score, all right." He flipped ash with a jerk of the wrist, concerned as hell about Mulholland and showing it. "Lander's a better bet—far better, in my opinion— than banking on any of your sharpshooters to be plumb certain he's picking the right man. They're good to have out there, sure. Just in case, sure . . . But what with the conditions, and the time they'll have to decide and all, it's going to be one helluva responsibility. They'll need a lead, and there's nothing to beat close quarters."

7:29 P.M.

ROBERTO OLIVARES was going from floor to floor, room to room. Incredibly, Shelley's was still functioning. More incredibly, there were people who expected nothing less. By now, accustomed to whole litanies of complaint, he almost dreaded presenting himself as a target for more.

He knocked and waited, passkeys ready in case nobody came: 229 this time.

"Good evening," he said as the door was opened by an elderly woman. "I am the manager, Roberto Olivares, and I regret having to inform you that, for a precaution, you must leave here not later than eight o'clock and make your way to the dining room."

"I see."

"We are being forced to keep the hotel in a state of absolute blackout until such a time as the gunman has gone. . . . So we are arranging for every single person to be in the safety of the dining room." He used his hands and shoulders, very telling. "All this is greatly regretted, believe me. But we are directed by the police, you understand. . . ."

"I see." No rudeness, no protestation. A wrinkled smile instead. "I doubt if you remember me, Mr. Olivares. I have stayed at Shelley's in the past most happily, and I really do wish to compliment you on the marvelous way you have managed to cope in the middle of what must be an extremely difficult and dangerous situation."

"It is nothing." Roberto Olivares flashed his best trained smile. "It is nothing at all," he said, glad as could be Helen wasn't there to hear.

7:36 P.M.

"RENATA?"

The hardest thing in all the world would be telling her. She was alone with Mary Kay when he arrived, Sam O'Hare just gone for the fourth time, and both of them looking drawn from the burdens of the day, the air stale with cigarette smoke and every ashtray piled with stubs.

"Hi, Harry," she said, offering a smile as he crossed the room, her own trauma over and done with; that, at least.

"There's something you must hear about." He'd forced the moment on himself and he dreaded her reaction; she was so emotional. "Something I've been asked to do."

"Like what?"

Maybe he should have been less blunt. "It . . . it's been put to me that I'm the one who should go and join Ralph Mulholland."

She stared at him as if she didn't quite comprehend. "You?"

"That's right."

"Why you?"

"They figure I'm the best qualified."

"How d'you mean—qualified? Qualified in what way?"

Her eyes hadn't left him. Alarm was in them now, pin points of fear, growing. How little we need words, he thought. He took her by the shoulders.

"Grattan's insisting on having one more person in there with him by not later than eight-thirty."

She nodded. "You, though." She couldn't accept it. "*You* . . ."

"Someone has to go."

"Oh Jesus," she said, her expression changing, almost hostile for a moment. She turned impulsively on Mary Kay. "Did you hear? Did you hear what Harry just said?"

He was glad Mary Kay was there: better, far better, than having Dannahay. "Cool it, will you," he began, "and listen to me. . . . There's a job to be done and—"

"What job?"

"Grattan's asked for certain items to be taken in."

"I know about that."

"Well, that's the job." He couldn't bring himself to mention anything more. She'd go up the wall if she knew. "McConnell and Dannahay have put their heads together and, among other things, they figure I'll be acceptable to Grattan. Less likely to make him jumpy than a total stranger, for instance. And I'm the right sort of build, close to what he's stipulated."

How lame it sounded. Tears were running down Renata Lander's cheeks, and for an instant he pitied her. "Harry, Harry—haven't we had enough?"

"Renata, dear," Mary Kay said gently, moving to her side. "Honey . . ."

"It's going to be all right," Lander said.

"And Noel . . . What about Noel?"

"It's going to be all right." He didn't want a scene now, couldn't bear a scene. "Everything'll be taken care of."

"Oh Jesus," she said again. She could smell the whisky on his breath. "The last thing I ever thought—"

"Stop it, can't you?" He kept his voice low. He felt cornered somehow, trapped in more ways than he could grasp. "I'm not the one the sweat's on for." He glanced at Mary Kay and left the rest unsaid. "I didn't volunteer, Renata. But they've made out a case, and I'm prepared to go along with it. Which would you prefer—that I turn my back?" Again his eyes deserted her for Mary Kay, a reputation to restore, the future's possibilities already weighed. "I owe Ralph Mulholland this, I figure. This'll be a kind of quid pro quo. . . . Don't you see that?"

Outside, he noticed, the light had already started to fail.

7:50 P.M.

THE WARD SISTER came over to Yorke's bedside with the *Standard* and showed him the back-page photograph.

"You're famous, did you know?"

Yorke looked at himself being loaded on a stretcher into the ambulance and smirked self-consciously.

"Whatever happened to my cap?"

"Won't they give you another one, then?" She grinned at him, another day done, almost time to go off duty. Then she pointed an ultraclean fingernail at a single paragraph near the bottom of the page. "What d'you make of that? Looks like she tried to gas herself—a Mrs. Ruth Ireland, of Poole, Hampshire. Poole's where Richard Ireland lives, I'm sure. . . . Or do you suppose that's just a coincidence?"

THE HELICOPTER PILOT was younger than McConnell had thought he'd be. Quite unperturbed on the surface, but full of questions.

"Do I start my engines before the group reaches me, or after?"

"After," McConnell said. He wanted everything as quiet as possible. "As soon as we get a signal they're coming out, we'll flash you."

"Where from?"

"The Navy Building. Two flashes—dah, dah."

The caravan wasn't an ideal briefing room, not with so many pressing round; but it served. O'Hare, Ryder, Dannahay, Lander, the Commissioner, Llewellyn, the helicopter pilot, Savage's selected marksmen—all were there, over and above the manning staff. The rain bounced nonstop on the roof, and every so often a telephone rang or the teleprinter thudded.

McConnell pointed to Llewellyn's plan of the square. "When they leave the hotel, all the odds are they'll take the shortest route." He spoke as if Lander wasn't present. "This means Grattan will make them cross to the center of the square from the northwest corner—here, just past where the man was killed this morning." That seemed a lifetime ago now. McConnell finger-traced Grattan's most likely approach to the helicopter. "He'll be counting every step, and I can't see him going any other way."

"But if he does?"—the Commissioner.

"If he does, he'll still be covered when it matters most. All the paths converge." McConnell stroked fields of fire across the plan away from the chestnut and the elm where two of the three marksmen were to be positioned. "He can go whichever way he pleases. My bet, though, is that he'll make a beeline."

"Mine too," Dannahay agreed.

"They'll move at a walk—that, I would have thought, is a certainty. And we'll be able to hear them." McConnell darted a glance at Lander. "Drag your feet a bit, will you? Not obviously. Every so often a scuff or two." With a thumb jerked at the marksmen he explained: "These fellows will need to locate you as early as they can."

"Okay." Lander licked his lips.

"Don't take action until you're in this general area." Again McConnell pointed, roughing out a circle. "Seventy-five paces in from the roadway will bring you to it. You're past the trees by then, and there's only grass and paths and flower beds."

You, he was saying now, not they.

He turned back to those who would remain on the side lines. "Grattan's a sight too clever to throw his advantages away by being obvious and staying last in line or keeping immediately behind the Ambassador. His object is to confuse, and his insistence on identical disguises is an indication of the sort of countermeasures he expects from us. But it's absolutely no use our mounting searchlights around the square or anything conventional like that. A sudden flood of light and you still wouldn't be certain of your target."

He was addressing the marksmen. "Mr. Lander, on the other hand, will have the benefit of knowing exactly where Grattan has placed himself. And the success of this operation is going to depend on making use of the second or two's advantage he expects to gain by throwing Grattan with a surprise voice. Grattan's more susceptible to this kind of thing than most, and there's certain to be a telltale reaction—sufficient, whatever it is, to ensure identification and for you to give instant support to Mr. Lander."

Dannahay said: "Hadn't they better know what voice Harry's going to use?"

McConnell nodded and asked Lander: "What about that?"

"I'll do Bogart," Lander said.

"And you'll say—?"

"Now listen to me, sweetheart." Lander put on the voice. "Now listen to me, sweetheart." It was uncanny. No one laughed or smiled. They were grown men, and this had to do with life and death.

"No more'n that?" Dannahay said. " 'Now listen to me, sweetheart'—that all?"

"There won't be time."

"These covering guys'll need to hear you at about forty yards, so you'll have to speak up."

"Okay," Lander said.

"What happens," one of the marksmen wanted to know, "if you fail to pick up the gun from the door when you leave Shelley's?"

"I was coming to that," McConnell said. "It's a possibility we can't overlook."

"Does Mr. Lander go ahead with the impersonation?"

"Yes."

"The same impersonation?"

"That's right."

"In which case the onus will be completely on us?"

"Completely." McConnell paused. "I should mention that Mr. Lander is most anxious to be armed. But in the event of this proving impossible, he is nevertheless prepared to initiate the action which will enable you to select Grattan and pick him off."

He looked at the grave faces, grouped as if for a photograph, and in the seriousness of that moment it struck him just how courageous Lander would have to be.

"Now," he said, "are there any other questions?"

8:01 P.M.

"ATTENTION, attention, please . . . This is a police message. For emergency reasons, electricity supply to this area of Mayfair has been temporarily cut off. The district affected is centered on Grosvenor Square and is bordered by Green Street, Mount Street, Carlos Place, and Duke Street. . . . All those in the area are asked to be as patient as possible. Supply will be restored at the earliest possible opportunity. . . ."

The rain had eased a little and the leaden sky was tinged with pink. Noel Lander watched the police car vanish into Carlos Place and listened to the blown-up voice die in the distance. He had never been in this room before, the Ambassador's inner sanctum, with the flag mounted in the corner beside the big desk and the vivid blanket paintings and the wide-screen view of Grosvenor Square.

"D'you want a drink, Noel?" Mary Kay asked him.

"No, thanks."

He didn't feel sick exactly, but sort of queasy—pride and apprehension mixed. Everything had happened so fast. Hardly five minutes ago his mother had arrived at Bruton Mews with Mary Kay Mulholland and brought him straight here, explaining on the way.

He gazed out at the helicopter. A number of policemen were standing under trees in its vicinity and two Marine guards had just gone over from the Embassy, one of them carrying a valise.

"Know something, Noel?" Mary Kay came and stood beside him. "I couldn't tell your father this before he had to go. But he's a fine man, Noel. A real fine brave man." Close to, her face was terribly tired-looking. "And when this is over we'll tell him so, huh? All three of us will tell him."

"You bet," he said, and put an arm around his mother's

waist, staring straight ahead and blinking the emotion away as best he could.

8:17 P.M.
"GRATTAN?" McConnell was using the phone in the night porter's cubicle. "I don't want any misunderstanding, Grattan."

"I'm listening."

"The third man will come to the door of the room in exactly thirteen minutes. At eight-thirty. He'll knock as before, same as the Ambassador." He could hear the heave of Grattan's breathing. "What he'll bring with him are wigs, overcoats, and a cardboard box in which you'll find one loaded Walther PP and three plastic revolvers. Plus a flashlight."

"Go on."

"The helicopter is standing by and the money's aboard. In addition, you will have heard the street announcement about the blackout. . . . Now, if that isn't co-operation, Grattan, I don't know what is. And I've collaborated because of the people you've got in there with you. They're not to be harmed, d'you hear? There's a limit to how far you can use them. I want no misunderstanding. I need to have one thing from you in return."

"Such as?"

"Some idea of when you're coming out." McConnell waited for seconds on end, no real hope in the waiting, just chancing it. "For their sake. An approximation will do. It'll be dark within the hour, and they're tired . . . hungry."

"I'll come when I'm good and ready," Grattan threatened, "and not bloody before."

8:26 P.M.

"GOOD LUCK," McConnell said with some passion.

"Thanks."

Dannahay managed an indecipherable sort of grin. "Same from me, Harry." Then he said: "Some feather in your cap, eh?" He was so sure nothing would go wrong.

He shook hands with Lander and helped to load him with the stuff he was to carry. All the hotel guests had been shepherded into the dining room, out of harm's way, and it was dusky now in the empty foyer, not easy to be certain about a person's expression.

"There's one last thing about the gun."

"Yeah?"

Six times Lander had rehearsed lifting it from the inside of the door handle as he went by—using his left hand, the dummy pistol held in his right. And it was easy; eyes shut and it was easy.

"Make sure you pull it up into your sleeve as soon as you palm it." *When,* not *if.* "At once, understand? Hide it well away until you decide to take him."

"Sure."

Lander was sweating; despite the gloom it showed. And the breath of whisky was on him still; but stale now, a good hour since he'd taken any. He looked sharp enough, very clear about what he was doing.

Dannahay said: "Get Mulholland off the hook for us, Harry."

"Sure."

There was nothing to say after that. McConnell followed Lander into the elevator, and Dannahay watched as the doors trundled across.

DARKNESS

8:30 P.M.

INSTINCT took over from reason the moment Lander parted
from McConnell and Savage and started along the fifth-floor
corridor alone. Because of the load he was carrying he didn't
see the warning scatter of corn flakes or the tray that Gabrielle
Wilding had never collected. Alarm froze into his neck hair
as he stumbled across them in the shrunken light. For an
instant the temptation was to turn about and run, weakness
like a swift breeze in his belly, but he mastered it and the
moment passed, leaving his heart thudding.

He knocked as instructed, three clear raps. They would
have known he was there without that, but even so he had
to wait. The wad of tissue was pulled out of the splintered
hole in the door, and for several seconds he felt himself
observed. Then, and only then, was the bolt drawn and the
door pulled inward.

The raw smell of the room was unlike anything he had
ever known, compounded of the sweat of private agonies and
the day-long hopes of survival and triumph and salvation.
Lander's nostrils flared as he entered and stood there in the

semidarkness. The door was closed hard behind him, shapes and shades of shadow everywhere, someone sitting, someone standing, the curtains drawn. Something prodded into him, and his body was searched, swiftly, expertly, all done in seconds. Then Grattan spoke.

"Give me the flashlight."

It was snatched from him. A moment afterward the beam was switched on, full in his face. "God," he heard Mulholland exclaim. But Grattan said: "What's your height?"

"Around five ten."

The beam flicked up and down distrustfully, head to toe. "Put all that stuff on the floor and give me the box."

Lander obeyed, determined to obey, here to do nothing else until the moment came. The beam was still directed into his eyes as Grattan continued to look him over.

"How many in the corridor out there?"

"None." McConnell and Savage would have left by now.

"Lie to me and you'll regret it. . . . You seen the helicopter?"

"Yes."

As if it were an accusation Grattan then said: "I know you. . . . I know your voice."

Sound, smell, taste, touch—these were still the keys to his faulty defense system. Lander nodded, an unreasoning panic stopped in its tracks: Grattan continued to rely on what he heard.

"I'm Harry Lander."

Grattan snorted, peering from behind the bright disc of the flashlight. "You got a nerve," he said, big whites to his eyes. "You got a fucking nerve, all right."

Then he laughed, a jerked-out noise, soon done. Lander said nothing, mind flitting. The beam was off his face now, and he could just about see Ireland and Mulholland. Ireland was sitting with his head in his hands, but Mulholland acknowledged him, surprise still showing. Everyone was in shirt sleeves and the room was a shambles, glass and broken bric-a-brac lying around.

"Seen Mary Kay?" Mulholland asked, quick and quiet, like a man behind bars.

"She's fine . . . just fine."

Grattan shone the flashlight into the cardboard box and grabbed the Walther PP. He checked the magazine and worked the action, the rifle balanced in the crook of his arm. Then he test-fired the pistol into the wall, no warning. Satisfied, he went into the bathroom, backing in, taking no chances, and spilled all the rifle shells down the toilet, the bolt after them. Finally he let the rifle fall and came out, locking the door, pocketing the key.

"On the bed," he ordered Lander. "Over there with Mulholland."

He crossed to the chair he'd used all day and perched himself, flashlight in one hand, pistol in the other. The beam found Lander's face again, dazzling.

"Lander . . . Bloody Lander."

He stared, trying to piece the tatters of his memory together, still not entirely convinced. And Lander took heart from what he saw, less panicky about the weapon he would use than he had suddenly begun to feel. Another voice now and Grattan would have dropped his guard the way Dannahay said.

Yes . . . *Yes.*

8:46 P.M.

McCONNELL TAPED the pistol for Lander into position on the inside of the heavy door handle while Dannahay watched, holding a cigarette lighter close and shielding the jet of flame with the other hand. Dark was settling fast now, distances contracting all the time, the quiet intensifying.

McConnell stood back a little, silent on the thick pile. One strand of tape was enough. "What d'you think?"

"I'd say it's okay." Dannahay made as if to lift the pistol away, arm bent at the elbow. "Yeah, yeah"—he nodded—"that's great."

"Cigarette?"

"Thanks."

Eighty people, guests and staff, were shut in the dining room with Helen and Roberto Olivares. The rest of Shelley's was empty, the switchboard closed down, Dannahay and himself about to leave. And he ached in every muscle, in the bone even.

"Reckon he'll pull it off?" All of a sudden there were doubts, fatigue and strain feeding them.

"Don't see why not."

"We had to gamble somewhere, seems to me. And I'd rather it was here than at Heathrow. Much rather." He was thinking aloud. "Once you've submitted to the first lift-off, you're faced with another."

"That's right."

"And the more dragged out a situation's allowed to get, the more likely it is that something'll go snap."

"That's right," Dannahay said again. He made a small adjustment to the angle at which the pistol was fastened, bending close. "Couldn't agree more."

The glass doors were wide open, wedged back on their catches. There were six steps down into North Audley Street, and McConnell and Dannahay took them in the gloom, turning right, walking quietly. Grattan would come this way.

"I hate the idea of killing," McConnell admitted, flicking a half-spent cigarette into the gutter. "Even when it's necessary. Even then."

"Know just how you feel," Dannahay agreed, pace for pace beside him. "But sometimes it's the only way."

The rain had slackened quite a bit within the last hour, but it still made them tighten up their eyes.

8:52 P.M.

THE FOUR WIGS were in neat cellophane pouches. Grattan tossed three of them across the room. "Put 'em on," he said, "and let's have a look at you."

They were full head pieces, dark brown, the hair thick and slightly waved. Even at close quarters their effect was remarkable. Mulholland's grey sideburns were the principal giveaway, but then Mulholland was already the odd man out, shorter and burlier.

Grattan nodded as he studied them, pleased with himself. "Now the overcoats."

It was anyone's guess where he'd got the idea, but it certainly achieved what he was after. Even in the direct glare of the flashlight, Lander and Ireland had taken on a degree of sameness, and with their collars up and their heads turned that way and this the loss of personal identity was even more marked. In blackout, and at distance, it would surely be total.

"Get hold of the guns."

Mulholland passed an imitation revolver to each of the others—a replica Smith and Wesson, almost indistinguishable from the real thing except for its lightness.

"Hold 'em like you're covering someone."

The black snouts stuck out of their hands, Lander's the same as the others. The overcoat sleeves were quite long, too long on Mulholland, sartorial blemishes that would go unnoticed.

"Good," Grattan muttered. "That's good." He dragged a forearm across his face. "Okay—now sit."

They did so, looking like strangers, darting glances at one another, powerless and uneasy. He kept the flashlight on them, though not always on their faces. After a while he got to his feet and went across to the window, stared out and returned, the wig and overcoat he would use himself still lying where Lander had put them down when he entered.

Mulholland said: "When do we go?"

Grattan ignored him.

"Soon?"

No answer. Ireland began to tremble again, and Lander could feel the vibration through the bed. He was surprised; he didn't know, hadn't realized. And it wasn't a thing he wanted to know, not there and then. He needed to keep as calm as he could. He sat between Ireland and Mulholland and tried to put blinkers on his mind, concentrating on what he had come to do—at the door downstairs, in the square.

And why: because of before and after.

9:03 P.M.

HELEN OLIVARES addressed the dark buzzing all around her in the dining room.

"Ladies and gentlemen . . . How long we are going to be here I cannot say. Once again my husband and I offer the management's apologies for what is, of course, a quite unparalleled situation. Appalling too—that goes without saying; and heading towards a climax as I speak. Some of our guests, perhaps not unnaturally, have chosen to leave. To those of you who have not so chosen may I just say that we most sincerely trust that the upheaval and inconvenience you have suffered during the day will not prejudice you against returning to Shelley's on future occasions. . . . Now, the police will advise us the moment the emergency is at an end. Meanwhile, they say, we should remain as quiet as possible and not in any way be alarmed for ourselves. . . ."

Incredible woman, Roberto Olivares thought. *Fantastic*.

"I'm going to join the SPG man at the memorial," Dannahay muttered. "Any objection?"

McConnell shook his head.

"Where you going to be yourself?"

"By the chestnut."

Of the marksmen's agreed positions he reckoned the chestnut was closest to the area in which Lander would make his move. And it was imperative to be close, close as could be. Seconds would decide when the time came, and Lander was going to need all the support he could get.

McConnell asked: "How good are you at the waiting bit?"

"Waiting's been the story of my life," Dannahay confessed, "but I don't get any better at it. . . . *Ciao*."

The darkness swallowed him up almost as soon as they parted.

A policeman flattened into the doorway of the deserted Sin Nombre restaurant and used his personal radio to report.

"Nothing yet." He was forty yards from Shelley's and looking past it toward Grosvenor Square, already forced to rely on his hearing. "Not a blind thing."

9:16 P.M.

No SOUND of the rain on the window now.

Grattan said suddenly: "How was it when you came in? Getting worse? Getting better?"

"Getting better," Lander answered. "Easing."

Grattan craned his neck, looking out, nothing to be seen except the horizon's cloud glow, pink and diffused. He jerked the curtains into an overlap and switched the flashlight back on, propping it on a bedside table so that the beam reflected off the ceiling.

The fourth wig and overcoat were still untouched, but the signs were that he wouldn't delay for long. There was enormous tension in him, transmitted to the others. The sight of them, demeaned and disguised, seemed all the time to be urging him to act. Every one of his demands and conditions had been met: outside, the silence beckoned and the darkness was waiting. And yet, despite his near readiness, a gambler's indecision had come over him. When he finally herded them out of this room, making for the street five floors below and the helicopter in the center of the nearby square, it would be as irrevocable as walking the plank, three hundred and more paces like so many miles, eyes everywhere, enemies.

"Stand up," he told them with parade-ground abruptness. "On your feet."

They looked so alike, even Mulholland, only a couple of inches in it.

"You," Grattan said to Lander. "Which one are you?"

"Lander."

"Get in line with Mulholland. In front of him."

Lander frowned, his mind racing. *In front?*

"And you"—to Ireland—"come alongside. On Mulholland's right . . . There, yes." He stepped in behind them all, the Walther touching Mulholland's back. "Now turn," he ordered Ireland, "and face inward." They were no more than arm's length from each other. "And you up front—"

"Yes?"

"Turn yourself around."

Lander swung about to face Mulholland. Grattan had taken the very position McConnell had argued was unlikely.

"Now raise the guns. Bring 'em up waist high—all of you."

He moved off to the side and studied them, apparently

satisfied with what he saw, one corner of his mouth twitching. Somebody's guts rumbled.

"This is how we'll go out of here. Three in line, one at the side. All the way you'll keep the same formation, you on the right turned inward at Mulholland, you in front facing back at him, all of you staying close."

Lander said: "I walk backward?"

"How else?" Grattan stood at another viewpoint, eying them critically, their voices for him like distinguishing footnotes. "Mulholland—you'll take the flashlight. Shine it down at your feet while we're on the stairs. Nowhere else except at your feet. Drop it when I tell you. Understand?"

Mulholland nodded. When Grattan was right behind him just now he had almost nerved himself to go for the gun with a fierce backward chop, spinning simultaneously and following in with fists and feet. Almost. For a second he'd been that close to trying—and his spine knew the chill of it even now. As fast as light he remembered the nail file he'd hesitated over in his office before giving himself up to this demented man and thought how he might have been able to use it—in the eyes, in the neck. But the moment passed and his recklessness died a death.

Someone else must end this for them. God knows how, but someone outside would have to do it. That's what they were there for.

"We'll take it slowly," Grattan was saying, as if to colleagues. "And everyone points his gun at the one in the middle, at Mulholland. All the time, see?"

He picked up the overcoat and put it on, after which he dragged the wig over his head. It made him look younger, despite the wild and sunken eyes, but to those with the night-sight rifles he would appear impossibly like the others.

"Now listen to me, sweetheart . . ." Lander heard the Bogart phrase repeating inside his head, and he thought of Noel, then Renata, then Dannahay; in that order. "Now listen to me, sweetheart . . ." He did these things for fun, as a game, but this was no game. This was his day of obligation.

Then he started to think about himself, and a stream of sweat began to pump out of him. All at once the room seemed almost like a place of safety.

9:23 P.M.

O'HARE said angrily: "I wish to God we'd dug our toes in twelve hours ago. Weakness never pays." He was all nerves, pessimistic and cantankerous. "If my argument had been listened to this morning, Ralph would never have gotten himself into this terrible situation."

"And one or two hostages might well be dead as a result," Ryder retorted. "Ralph knew exactly what he was doing—and so did Lander. Both of them knew darned well."

"I still say Grattan's running a bluff."

"What's your worry, then?" He was indignant. "It's easy to take that line when you're out of range of the consequences."

"Now look here—"

"Forget it, Sam. I'm sorry, but don't go on about it. And if the setup out there in the square is what you call weakness, then I'm a Hottentot."

They were in the lobby beside the Ambassador's office, just themselves, the strain doing damage to them both. No lights, not a glimmer. They groped their way past desks and chairs to the inner door.

"Mary Kay?"

"Hi."

They might as well have had blindfolds on. "Mrs. Lander here?"

"And Noel," she said.

They all came together, five of them, touching the window

to be sure they had reached it and peering into an extension of the darkness that all but hid them from themselves.

O'Hare said: "Any signal from the Navy Building?"

"Not yet."

Every window that overlooked Grosvenor Square was inhabited like this, people in their hundreds staring into what remained of the rain, crowding every viewpoint, sharing the drama on their doorstep with the newsmen of the world. But here there was no small talk, no attempts to kill time. The boy and the two women had gone beyond that, all their reserves sucked dry, no point in voicing hopes: and prayers were private. Dear God, Noel was saying silently, let my dad be okay. And Mr. Mulholland . . .

"Come on," O'Hare murmured tersely. "For Pete's sake."

9:28 P.M.

"RIGHT," Grattan decided. "We go now."

What made him choose that moment they would never know. Perhaps it was the rain; the more it eased, the less it was to his advantage. Four times since he'd stood them in line he had returned to the window, and each time Lander was sure it would make up his mind.

"Listen," Grattan said, suddenly as cold as ice. "I got everything to gain and nothing much to lose. So think about it. Mulholland's a dead man the moment any one of you fancy you can trick me."

He swept them with his glare, and Ireland couldn't meet it, quite ruined now, an empty cipher, no Nick Sudden to the rescue.

"Stay close. Keep your collars up and the guns pointed. And something else—you in front, you, Lander . . . The shortest way, mind. Go to the middle of the street outside and make it straight from there. Mulholland will aim you right."

He passed the flashlight to Mulholland, who shone it at the floor. Grattan backed past them to the door and slid the bolt. Then he stood aside and swung the door open, silence greeting them, blackness, an awful sense of expectancy like something waiting on tiptoe. They weren't out of the room yet and already it was there.

"Move," Grattan breathed.

He stepped into line as Mulholland went by. They shuffled and clattered through the crispies and coffee cups, Lander backward, no faltering this time. The light made a shifting pool at Mulholland's feet, little reflection off the red-and-black-patterned carpet, semidarkness from the waist up. They could hear the brush of each other's clothing, the tiny squeak of a shoe. It seemed cooler in the corridor, and the cooped-up stink had gone from the air. Lander kept twisting his head round, slowing as he came near to where he thought the stairs began. A minute must have passed before he reached them, and twice Mulholland shunted into him, Ireland another time, everyone stiff and clumsy and scared.

On the stairs their difficulties increased. They stumbled after one another, clutching the handrail, shoulders brushing the wall. Nine faltering steps down, then a half-turn and nine more, another turn and nine more: Lander counted, backing away from Mulholland, Ireland close in, the three of them crowded from the rear, Grattan pressing forward with the Walther prod-prodding against the small of Mulholland's back.

None of them knew what Lander knew, so theirs were different fears from his—at every turn, at every step, with every groping second. Each time they reached the level of a lower floor and regrouped by the elevator doors they instinctively expected countermeasures, especially there, invisible corridors to either side of them, Mulholland's senses cringing away from the nearness of the gun, Ireland's teeth clenched and his mind engulfed by a soundless screaming.

"Keep on!"

Grattan's sharp whisper gave no real clue to where he was positioned: at shoulder height the dark had little shape, and their faces were lost in it, virtually identical. Shadows swirled and lumped passing distortions of themselves together while the sound of their breathing and the repeated squeak of leather kept pace with them.

Lander had counted the floors as well as the steps, and there was only one to go now. One more, and then the foyer and the doors out into the street; *and the pistol.*

They came on down, quadruplets, the small guns pointing, Grattan at their heels. The last flight curled in a long sweep, and they stepped in and out of the jerking splash of light. Sick with nerves, Lander finished with the staircase and paused for the rest to bunch up, the cavernous expanse of Shelley's foyer all around them as they stood within the circle of the flashlight's beam.

Then Grattan breathed: "Put it out." Blackness covered them instantly. "Drop it." They heard its cushioned thud. "Move," the order was, and they moved, close together, as if for mutual protection.

"Nothing," the constable reported softly from the Sin Nombre doorway. "Nothing yet."

Lander's fear was that he would bungle it. In the instant before Mulholland killed the light he managed a mental alignment with the door he wanted, but he couldn't sustain it for long and the foyer seemed endless. As his eyes adjusted, one area of the darkness took on a slightly different texture; straining round he could vaguely identify the rectangular shape of the entrance. He gulped in a breath and altered course, Mulholland catching his feet as he did so. He could just make out Mulholland's bulk, but Grattan he couldn't see at all.

Dribbles of sweat burst from under his wig, and he blinked them desperately away. "Now listen to me, sweetheart"—to speak it without being armed himself would require the most enormous act of faith. Getting the pistol was vital; crucial.

He shortened his backward stride, head turned, the dark somehow solidifying to the sides of him. He edged off line a shade more, reaching across his body until the fingers of his left hand touched glass. Encouraged he felt along the surface of the door, slowing again but not quite halting. He'd rehearsed the snatch walking forward, but in the end this wasn't all that different.

Now . . . *Now.*

Suddenly what he wanted was there, the handle as big as a discus, and his fingers tightened around the pistol butt at the back of it. There was a tiny ripping sound as the tape gave way, but that was all, and it could have been anything. In almost the same instant the overcoat sleeve was down over Lander's hand, and relief flushed through him like a torrent of fire.

"What's your name?" Dannahay asked the sharpshooter stationed at the base of the Roosevelt statue.

"Booker."

They weren't all that far from the helicopter, but he couldn't see it; couldn't see anything. And the rain was hardly a drizzle now.

As they emerged into North Audley Street the sense of being waited for was there again. Grattan pressed from behind, and Lander groped cautiously in front, shuffle-shuffle into the night, tight together, feet feeling for the steps. They descended them in ragged fashion, blind men, bumping each other on the sidewalk, controlled as always by the threat of Grattan's gun.

"They're outside. . . . They're on their way"—from the Sin Nombre to the caravan, from the caravan to the Navy Building, two winking signal flashes from the Navy Building to those in Grosvenor Square.

In the time this took they covered a dozen paces, finding the roadway, changing direction. A narrowing trench of light glittered beyond the blackout zone—Orchard Street, Baker Street; in the distance life went on, madness and terror here, only here. They began to pick up a sort of rhythm, slow and scuffling, the sky just sufficiently lighter than the flanking façades to help keep them on course.

Beneath his left sleeve Lander shifted the pistol's safety catch. A sudden side step now and he could probably take Grattan. No need for Bogart, no need for the waiting marksman. The thought trembled in mind and body, tempting him, scaring him. Grattan was only three or four yards away, but he remained invisible, and the least miscalculation could mean disaster. Better to wait, Lander knew. No one would forgive him if he blundered something on his own and Mulholland paid for it. Stick to the plan. Wait until the marksmen had them in their special sights and Bogart could give them the all-important clue.

He backed away all the time from what he could see of Mulholland, his right hand pointing the plastic revolver, Mulholland pointing one at him, Ireland one at Mulholland, Grattan close behind with the real thing. Twice he deliberately scraped his heels, doubts and panic compounded, momentarily convinced that no one knew they were at large in North Audley Street at all.

The taste of sickness rose in his throat. *For Christ's sake,* he warned himself feverishly, *do what was said—how and when and where.*

———

"This is Robert Armitage, BBC, and word has just reached me that they are out of Shelley's Hotel and making towards Grosvenor Square. At this very moment, as I speak to you from a second-floor vantage point in the Navy Building, they are somewhere in the absolute darkness of the street below me. . . . This means that about two hundred yards separate them from the waiting helicopter, which is the gunman's immediate objective. For those of us even this close to the drama the tension is practically unbearable; but for Ambassador Ralph Mulholland and Richard Ireland and the third hostage, Harry Lander, the reality of what they are being forced to endure has long since had about it an infinitely more terrible dimension. . . ."

9:41 P.M.
AT GROUND LEVEL the night remained without shape, almost impenetrable. But as the minutes passed, the sky slowly separated itself a little more from everything else, and Lander could see from its expanse that they had done with North Audley Street and were entering the northwest corner of the square.

Most of the way they had maintained an untidy compactness, but now for a while they began to falter again, Ireland twice boring in as if he were drunk, Mulholland changing step like a rookie. Upper Brook Street offered a distant glimpse of an illuminated Park Lane, numbingly unreal as a bus showed bright as a new red toy. Over his shoulder Lander began to make out the lofty bulk of trees and he could hear the soft soggy hiss of rain on foliage. Just then his heels struck a curb, and he realized he was across onto the sidewalk where, on the one hand, the parking meters were, and, on the other, a hedge surrounded the memorial gardens.

Another sixty or seventy paces and he would have reached the area McConnell had circled on the sketch. They were that close now.

"I can hear them," McConnell whispered suddenly.

The marksman he was with leaned against the wet bark of the chestnut and leveled the rifle, squinting into the big tunnel of the night sight.

"How 'bout you?" McConnell pressed him.

"I can see them."

Lander had fumbled his way along the outside of the hedge until he reached the tarmac pathway leading like the spoke of a wheel to where the helicopter waited. For the last time he did as he'd been asked and scuffed his feet, and then he slowed until he was as sure as he could be that Grattan was in line behind Mulholland and Ireland alongside.

The rain dripped off the trees here, heavy as bird droppings, and the front of the wig was plastered down over his forehead. Lander started backing along the pathway, counting the paces, the pistol still hidden in his sleeve. A dangling spray of leaves clawed across his face, making him start, every sense at fever pitch. The marksmen would have sighted them by now, trigger fingers on first pressure, McConnell waiting, Dannahay waiting. . . . The thought stroked his spine.

Thirty or forty yards more. There was a sound like surf in his ears, as if he were beginning to drown, a mounting sense of panic with it, images of things past filling his frightened mind's eye, the Libyan suddenly centered there, last night at the Vagabond, other nights, other contacts.

"Now listen to me, sweetheart . . ." Soon, very soon.

He peered beyond the bulky closeness of Mulholland, searching for Grattan, but in vain; it was that dark. In the same moment his feet missed the narrow path and he slipped a little, faltering, alarm clenched like a fist in his guts in case one of the marksmen made something of it and let fly.

There were trees above them still, but now he could smell the sodden horse dung piled on the rose beds, so the open space was only just behind him. He seemed almost stupefied by this time, out of reach of himself in some way, everything he ever was and could be once again all swamped by what was about to happen.

Ten paces . . . A dozen times faster than speech, he thought of Renata and Noel and wondered fleetingly where they were. Ten paces, nine, eight . . . He was close to the marksmen now, about to put his trust in them. Seven, six, five . . . No trees suddenly, shuffle-shuffle like marionettes, all alike. Four, three, two . . .

He sucked in air, mouth gone dry, and made his move— three swift sidelong steps to his right over the grass, the gun drawn quickly from his sleeve.

"Now listen to me, sweetheart."

He said it loud, in fear and with disbelief, but it was Bogart, all right; a good one. Mulholland went on past him, and for the first time since leaving Shelley's he really saw Grattan— motionless, bewildered, undeniably at bay.

Selected, singled out.

He fired at what was there, and as he did so a muzzle flash stabbed away to Grattan's far side. Close to, he heard an atrocious grunt, hideous and unnerving, and simultaneously part of the darkness seemed to change shape, falling, sinking down.

Lander recorded each impression in a kind of shocked slow motion—most vivid of all being the discovery that the pistol he had used bore a tiny luminous patch on the barrel, a single spot, no more than a bead.

"Take him, Booker," Dannahay jerked to the sharpshooter by the Roosevelt plinth. "The one with the mark." The night

221

sight showed it bright as a guiding star. "That one, yeah, yeah. *Take him!*"

Lander never heard this. There was chaos all around him, men running, men shouting, but the startled question beginning to swell in his mind was why the pistol was marked at all. Then Booker's shot cut him down and put an end to a dawning moment of astonished terror.

McConnell was the first to reach the area. He came with Savage, fast but wary. Grattan was still breathing, but he wasn't a danger any more, and McConnell disarmed him.

Savage said: "Mr. Lander's been hit, sir."

"God Almighty."

"He's *dead,* sir." It had the ring of complaint as well as confusion: until seconds ago the focus had been on Grattan, only Grattan.

McConnell picked up the gun from where it had fallen on the grass. He turned away from Lander, appalled and shaken, looking for Dannahay. Someone had a flashlight on now, and there was the hum of voices, sharp with alarm. Dannahay came at the double across the sopping grass, and McConnell didn't wait for him to arrive.

"Lander's been shot. . . . Killed."

"*Lander?*"

"From your position."

"That's not possible."

"And look at his gun. Look at *this.*" Even when thrust close, the small fluorescent spot on the barrel was only palely visible to the naked eye. "My man said it was like a beacon."

In a tone of great and sudden distress Dannahay said: "Shit. Aw, *shit.*"

"How'd it get there, for Christ's sake?"

"I put it on so as to help Lander as he came past the door out of Shelley's."

"You?"

"As an aid. Just for him."

"Who gave you the right—"

"No one else would have seen it. Only the one on the look-out for what was on the reverse side of the door handle. Only Lander . . . That was the idea."

"*Your* idea."

"Yes, but—"

"And then what happened?"

"I made a mistake, that's what happened."

"Only then?"

"I got Booker all confused, that's what happened."

McConnell said icily: "You expect me to believe this?"

A minute later Mulholland heard Dannahay repeating to McConnell: "Booker's in no way at fault, no way at all. The blame's mine, David; mine and mine alone."

He seemed shattered. It was eerie out there with the flash-lights shining down, flicking this way and that. Eerie, too, how alike the crude disguises still made Lander and Grattan look. Grattan groaned, and Savage knelt at his side, but Lander uttered no sound at all and never would again. From all parts of the square windows could be heard being opened, and small lights began to show. A general murmuring rose through the falling hiss of the rain. Another flashlight appeared on the front steps of the Embassy, and more people came hurrying— Noel and Renata Lander and Mary Kay Mulholland among them, calling as they ran, calling with hope, on the very brink of relief and laughter.

But Grattan had served his purpose. And what happened after that made Grosvenor Square a cruel and awful place to be.

10:52 P.M.

DANNAHAY walked with Knollenberg, anticlockwise round the square. Round and round, heads down, hands deep in pockets. The rain had finally stopped, and the street lights were all back on, the roadway and the sidewalks shining. No helicopter in front of the Roosevelt statue any more, no bodies on the grass by the rose beds, the screaming and the sobbing gone away. It was quiet now, as if none of this had ever been, as if Lander and Grattan had never lived.

And Knollenberg said: "When did you decide?"

"The moment I heard that Grattan was asking for another man." Dannahay flipped his fingers. "There and then."

"You were taking one hell of a risk."

"Risk's the nature of the game—Lander's and ours both. We all but had him, as it was. We'd have sewed it up tonight in any case. This way he did his country a service."

He was talking about an operation that had been successfully terminated, a black operation; no need to spell out to the younger man what Lander had been doing, unnecessary to stress the nature and extent of his treason and the methods he had used to communicate with his Arab paymasters. Knollenberg knew all about that. But what he still hadn't fully grasped was the level of sanction under which Dannahay operated.

"Couldn't we have waited?" Knollenberg asked. "Couldn't we have netted him the way we'd planned?"

"Sure," Dannahay said. "But there's a limit to the amount of truth they can take back home. They've had their fill of scandals and betrayal—don't you reckon? On top of everything else this year and all."

They walked on a little. A few stars were beginning to show, bright as could be in the rain-washed air. The police had taken their barriers down, and the curious were coming into the square to stare at anything that remained of what had been done to other people.

"Failures are public," Dannahay said. "Didn't you know? Victories are private."

"How private?"

"You and me for a start."

"How about McConnell?"

"Gonna have some stonewalling to do with McConnell."

"Not only with him, I'd say."

"Right."

"Stonewalling alone might not be enough," Knollenberg argued, learning all the time.

"Right again."

"So?"

"I'm for pastures new," Dannahay told him. "Up and away."

"When?"

"Real soon, Charles." He shot Knollenberg a glance. "Just in case you're toying with the wrong idea, let me tell you one thing more."

"Okay."

"I was in touch all along. I got appropriate approval."

Then Knollenberg said: "What price you asking for the Mustang?"